Sunny

Rishelle.

Nick

ELMO

LIZ

Be on the lookout for the next Raven Hill Mystery:

Case #3: Beware the Gingerbread House

EMILY RODDA'S RAVEN HILL MYSTERIES

#1: THE GHOST OF RAVEN HILL

#2: THE SORCERER'S APPRENTICE

SCHOLASTIC INC.

New York   Toronto   London   Auckland   Sydney
Mexico City   New Delhi   Hong Kong   Buenos Aires

No part of this publication may be reproduced, stored in a retrieval system, or transmitted in any form or by any means, electronic, mechanical, photocopying, recording, or otherwise, without written permission of the publisher. For information regarding permission, write to Permissions Department, Scholastic Australia, P.O. Box 579, Lindfield, New South Wales, Australia 2070.

ISBN 0-439-77915-4

Series concept copyright © 1994 by Emily Rodda
Text copyright © 1994 by Scholastic Australia

All rights reserved. Published by Scholastic Inc., 557 Broadway, New York, NY 10012, by arrangement with Scholastic Press, an imprint of Scholastic Australia.

SCHOLASTIC, APPLE PAPERBACKS, and associated logos are trademarks and/or registered trademarks of Scholastic Inc.

12 11 10 9 8 7 6 5 4 3 2   5 6 7 8 9 10/0

Printed in the U.S.A.   40

First American bind-up edition, October 2005

Contents

EMILY RODDA'S
RAVEN HILL MYSTERIES

#1: THE GHOST OF RAVEN HILL

Emily Rodda

SCHOLASTIC INC.

New York Toronto London Auckland Sydney
Mexico City New Delhi Hong Kong Buenos Aires

Contents

1

The beginning

"I'm starving! And I'm broke," moaned Tom. "Penniless. Cleaned out. Poverty-stricken. Destitute."

"Join the club," said Sunny.

"What's new?" Richelle yawned at the same moment.

Nick didn't say anything. But his scowl said plenty.

"If only we had part-time jobs —" I began. But they all groaned.

"There *aren't* any jobs, Liz. You know that," sighed Sunny.

"Don't be negative, Sunny Chan," Tom scolded, rolling his eyes. "You're forgetting. Queen Lizzie has magical powers. She's going to *make* us some jobs. Aren't you, Your Majesty?"

I opened my mouth to shout at him. And then, suddenly, I had my brilliant idea. The idea that was going to make us all some money. The idea (though I didn't know it then) that was going to put us all up to our necks in trouble!

"Yes," I said calmly. "That's just what I'm going to do. Make us some jobs."

Sunny started knotting herself into a complicated yoga pose. I think she'd given up on me.

Tom leaned his chin on his hand. "Speak, wise one," he begged earnestly.

I tried to ignore him.

"This is what we do," I said. "We *advertise* ourselves. As a group. We call ourselves something that'll attract attention. Like . . . say . . . Help-for-Hire. To make it clear we're here to help out people."

Nick sighed heavily.

"And we say we'll do anything," I said.

Tom raised his eyebrows and opened his mouth.

"Within reason," I added quickly. I could see he was going to say something stupid like: What about lion taming? Or drug smuggling?

"Liz Free's fourteen-day poverty plan!" Tom exclaimed in his best TV ad voice. "Buy now and achieve total destitution in weeks! Plus, you get a set of stainless steel headaches absolutely free!"

Nick, agreeing with Tom for once in his life, looked scornfully down his nose at me. Sunny said nothing. Richelle, of course, just yawned and went on checking her hair for split ends. My dog, Monty, was paying more attention than she was.

We were in the Glen at the time. That's the patch of forest next to the park down at the end of my block. We knew that soon it would be sold and torn apart. We felt bad about that.

In elementary school, our gang had played in the Glen. And now that we were at Raven Hill High, we still went there to talk. It was quiet, except for birds, and cool all year-round. People said it was haunted, but the Glen Ghost had never bothered us. Up till then, anyway. That problem was still to come.

I looked around at the kids sprawled on the ground. Tom, gangly and skinny, sketching as usual; Sunny, small and energetic, now doing leg stretches; clever, dark-eyed computer-whiz Nick, chewing a stick and looking at the sky; beautiful, oblivious Richelle, who had now moved on from her split ends to her fingernails.

"Well?" I demanded.

"So we spend a fortune on an ad and end up with dog walking and babysitting," sneered Nick, spitting out his stick.

I nearly lost my temper. "Well, we have to do something, Nick! Our school break starts at the end of next week. And other things will come in as well."

Nick looked disgusted. I racked my brains for interesting jobs. "You and Sunny and I can type, so there's that," I said. "Or someone having a party might want us to help clean up. Or say a recording company needed a group of kids to be extras in a music video. They could call us."

Richelle raised her eyes and blinked at me. I congratulated myself. The music video idea had been an inspiration.

"We may as well try it," she drawled. Then added, in case anyone thought she was too into it: "Nothing else to do."

She looked at her hands again. But I knew she wasn't really examining her nail polish. She was imagining herself being "discovered" on the set of the music video. "That girl over there," the director would be saying, "the one with the superb mane of hair and the beautiful eyes. Richelle, isn't it? Put her in front."

Typically, as soon as Richelle said okay, everyone else fell into line. It's infuriating, the way that happens. But I catch myself doing it, too. Maybe it's because Richelle is usually so cool and bored that you think well, if she wants to do something, it must be really worth doing.

"Do we advertise in the *Pen* or the *Star*?" asked practical Sunny.

"The *Pen*'s old-fashioned," said Nick.

"The *Star*'s garbage," sneered Tom.

They started arguing about the rival local newspapers. I was pleased. At least now they were fighting about *how* we'd go ahead, not *if*. My worries were over.

Or so I thought. In fact, of course, they were just beginning.

❂

We took ages to work out what to put in the ad, and especially what to call ourselves. Nick suggested a name made up of initials, but when Tom started getting silly and suggesting things like TWIRP (Totally Weird, Inane Rip-off Plus) and BUMS (Brainy, Useful, Muscled Stars), he gave up on the idea.

In the end, we settled on Help-for-Hire after all. But we added Inc. to the end of it. Nick said that would make us sound well organized, like a real business.

I finally wrote the ad on Wednesday, sitting under the apple tree at school with everyone else looking over my shoulder. "HELP-FOR-HIRE INC. Five responsible, mature teenagers . . ." I began.

Tom said that calling us responsible and mature was false advertising and we'd end up in jail. Nick said that while in Tom's case that was so, the rest of us would be okay. Then they started insulting each other and Sunny had to threaten to beat them both up before they'd stop. They knew she could do it, too. So they settled down, and I went on writing.

In the end, the ad read:

HELP-FOR-HIRE INC.

Five responsible, mature teenagers will tackle any jobs around your house, garden, shop, or business. Typing OK, computer OK, children and pets OK. Raven Hill area only. Cheap hourly rate. No job too small. We'll do anything!

I thought it sounded quite good.

We put my own phone number at the bottom. Nick and Tom didn't want the responsibility. Sunny has four older sisters, and her phone's always busy. And no one even thought of giving Richelle's number. She'd be just as likely to write messages on the back of an envelope or something, then wander off and forget all about them.

The ad was going to cost a fortune. Most of the money we scraped together was mine and Nick's. Sunny doesn't get much allowance because her mom already pays for gymnastics, tae kwon do, *and* yoga classes. Tom gets something from his parents every week, but he never saves any. No wonder, the way he eats. The school cafeteria could survive on Tom alone, I swear.

And the day after we had our talk in the Glen, Richelle had

spent every cent she had on a new top. The top was very bare and sexy. I guess she thought it would impress the music video director.

Luckily, I had a little money saved, and Nick did, too. Or maybe he got it from his mother. Nick's an only child, and he has his mom twisted around his little finger.

The others said they'd pay us back when jobs started coming in. I had a little twinge of doubt. What if no jobs came in? Then Tom's joke about Liz Free's poverty plan would be only too true. For me, anyway.

2

It pays to advertise

We'd finally decided to put our ad in the *Pen*. My dad said that since the *Star* started up, the old paper had lost quite a few advertisers. Both papers were free, and they survived only because of paid ads. So I said our money should go to the *Pen*.

Nick said I was just being lame, as usual. But Sunny reminded him that all the old ladies in Raven Hill trusted the *Pen*. They hadn't gotten used to the *Star* yet. And they were the ones who most often needed jobs done around their houses. Nick could see the sense in that, so he backed off.

But when Sunny and I saw the *Pen* building the next afternoon, I started to wonder if we'd made the right choice after all. There was graffiti all over the front, and someone had changed the RAVEN HILL PEN sign at the entrance to read RAVEN HILL PAIN. The only nice thing about the place was the colored-glass window above the door. And it looked out of place, like a jewel in a garbage dump.

As we opened it, the door shrieked as if a parrot was stuck in the hinges. Inside was a small room with grubby light green walls.

Opposite the door hung a framed, spotty sign that read THE PEN IS MIGHTIER THAN THE SWORD.

The office smelled of old paper and dust. It had a hard-looking visitors' bench, murky-colored carpet, a huge plastic palm tree in a pot, and two ancient desks.

Behind one desk sat a cross-looking woman who glared at us as though she had a lot of personal problems and we'd caused every one of them. Behind the other desk, a bored-looking girl with long red fingernails was chewing gum and typing on a computer, very slowly.

The woman narrowed her eyes at us. "Yes?" she snapped.

Sunny nudged me and I held out our precious money. "I — I called," I stuttered. "About an ad."

The woman clicked her tongue as if the whole thing was a plot set up just to annoy her. "Bring it here, then," she sighed, and held out an impatient hand.

I felt like turning around and walking out, but at that moment a door in the back of the office swung open.

"Miss Moss?" chirped a voice. A small man with a round face and a tangle of red curly hair popped his head around the door. He had worry lines on his forehead and his eyes looked tired, but he smiled shyly at us. The smile somehow reminded me of someone else.

"Oh, sorry," he said. "I didn't know anyone was here."

The crabby woman sniffed. "A small advertisement, Mr. Zimmer," she said, as though to warn him that we were no one important.

"Ah." The man smiled again and ventured into the room. "May I?" he said, and took the ad from me. He read it, his eyebrows gradually creeping up till they were lost in his curly hair. And then I realized why his smile was so familiar. It was just like Elmo Zimmer's smile.

Elmo was in our year at school. He was a bit of a loner. I remembered someone saying that his mother had died when he was little, and he lived with his dad. Mr. Zimmer must be Elmo's father.

Mr. Zimmer pursed his lips. There was silence for a moment, except for the clicking of the chewing-girl's fingernails on her keyboard. I exchanged glances with Sunny. Was there something wrong with the ad? Or was Mr. Zimmer a bit — odd?

"Fate, Miss Moss!" exclaimed Mr. Zimmer.

My heart skipped a beat. The cranky woman behind the desk looked even angrier than before. "Mr. Zimmer . . ." she began warningly.

"No, no, Miss Moss! Six bad apples don't make a barrelful!" Mr. Zimmer shook his fist, with the ad still in it, in the air. I decided it was time to leave. I felt for Sunny's hand and took a small step back, ready to make a break for the door.

"Watch out!" barked Miss Moss, and I nearly leaped into the air with fright.

"Watch the plant! It's fragile!" she said, pointing with a bony finger. I turned and saw the horrible plastic palm just behind me. It didn't look as though it could be damaged by anything less than a ten-ton truck.

Mr. Zimmer, ignoring all this, was doing a little dance on the murky carpet. He waved the ad and beamed, looking crazier than ever. "Five plus Elmo equals six," he chortled. The girl at the computer gazed at him, her mouth slightly open.

"Mr. Zimmer . . ." Miss Moss growled again. But he wouldn't be stopped.

"Kids," he crowed, "you've just landed your first job."

We stared at him. "What job?" asked Sunny finally.

"My job!" exclaimed Mr. Zimmer. He rubbed his hands together gleefully. "You're going to work for me!"

❂

Mr. Zimmer, it seemed, needed a team to home-deliver the *Pen* around Raven Hill every Thursday. The team he'd had, six sophomore kids, also from Raven Hill High, had gone over to the *Star*. And they'd gone without warning.

"She offered them twice what I paid, to dump me flat," he muttered, frowning all over his round face. "She's crazy."

"Who is?" I asked nervously. I still wasn't too sure about Mr. Zimmer.

"Sheila Star! The owner of the *Star*," Mr. Zimmer exploded. "She wants to buy the *Pen*, and because I won't sell, she's trying to ruin me. But I'll show her!"

"Mmm," murmured Miss Moss. She obviously didn't have much faith in Mr. Zimmer.

He calmed down a bit. "Anyway, don't you worry about that," he said. "Just be here next Thursday morning at five, and . . ."

Maybe he sensed our shock, because he stopped. "A five A.M. start's okay, isn't it?" he demanded.

"Oh . . . oh, yes!" I gulped. I couldn't imagine what Nick

would say about getting up in what he would consider the middle of the night. Let alone Richelle, who I'll bet hadn't seen a sunrise in her entire life.

"Good," said Mr. Zimmer, and suddenly became very efficient. "Miss Moss! Map please!"

Sighing, Miss Moss handed him a map of the area.

"Your routes are marked here. Or you can work out your own, if you like. I don't care, as long as the papers get out," said Mr. Zimmer. "Elmo — you know my son, Elmo?"

We nodded.

"Well, Elmo will join you. You pick up your first loads here. Your pickup points for extra copies are here, here, and here —" He pointed to crosses marked on the map. "Got that?"

"Sure." I glanced anxiously at Sunny. Her face was, as usual, calm.

Mr. Zimmer passed the map to her. "See you Thursday, then," he said. He absentmindedly stuffed our ad into his pocket.

"Um — our ad, Mr. Zimmer," I ventured, pointing.

"Oh!" He went pink, and pulled the paper out again, smoothing out the creases. "Yes. Ah — see to this, Miss Moss!"

"Certainly, sir," she answered sourly, as if to say, you don't fool me with all that "see to this" business. You're not a boss's bootlace.

We put our money on the desk and escaped from the office. Outside, we clutched each other and started to laugh.

"What a place!" giggled Sunny. "Why doesn't he fire that terrible Miss Moss? She's so *rude* to him!"

"Maybe she's blackmailing him or something," I said.

11

"Anyway, Help-for-Hire's got at least one job. I'll call Tom and tell him. You call Nick and Richelle."

"Oh, no," Sunny objected. "Think I'm crazy?"

So in the end, we decided to wait till the next day and tell them together. About the job. And the five o'clock start. That way Sunny'd be able to hold Nick down so he couldn't strangle me, and with her free hand she could catch Richelle when she fainted.

3

Ruby, Alfie, Elmo, and Pearl

My mother worries a lot. The deal I had with her about Help-for-Hire was that I'd only take jobs in Raven Hill, and that I wouldn't take any jobs without telling her first. That way, she thought, she could screen out any loonies or slave traders who might answer our ad.

When I got home, she was making dinner while my little brother, Pete, sat in the living room watching TV. Monty was watching with him. Monty loves TV.

I found Mom in the kitchen peacefully singing to herself over the chopping board.

"I've found a job for Help-for-Hire," she announced when she saw me.

"What?" I picked up some pieces of carrot from the board and started eating them. Why is it that carrots always taste so much better in little pieces?

"A Miss Plummer down at Golden Pines wants someone to run messages for her, and she wants to pay."

"How did she find out about us?" I asked in surprise, sneaking some more carrots.

"I was talking to the Golden Pines supervisor at the bank today," said Mom smugly, batting my hand away. "I told her about Help-for-Hire, and she told me about Miss Plummer."

"Wow! Thanks, Mom."

Golden Pines was this old people's home at the end of our block, right beside the Glen. How handy. I'd take that job myself.

Then I told Mom about the *Pen*. She approved. She said she'd heard Elmo Zimmer was a very nice man.

"Elmo's the son, Mom," I said patiently, watching her begin chopping the onions with her mouth open. (Mom had read a Home Hints column in a magazine that explained if you kept your mouth open, the onions wouldn't make your eyes water. So she always looked half-witted when she was chopping onions.)

"Yes, I know," said Mom. "The father died early this year. He was an old devil, they say."

This conversation was getting very strange. "Mr. Zimmer isn't dead, Mom," I said. "And Elmo's not a man. He's only in my grade."

She put down the knife and wiped her eyes. Maybe she hadn't kept her mouth open wide enough.

"Elizabeth, I wish you'd pay attention," she sighed, very unfairly I thought. "*Your* Elmo is *my* Elmo's son. And the old man was Elmo, too. Three generations. Three Elmo Zimmers. See?"

I nodded. Maybe.

"Anyway, when do you start?" asked Mom.

"Next Thursday," I said. "The day our ad goes in." I grabbed an apple, bit into it, and made for the door.

"Now you'll be very careful, won't you, Liz?" my mother said.

She was frowning. I could see that the mention of the ad had started her worrying again.

"Mom, don't worry," I said, with my mouth full. "A job with the local paper and one in an old people's home! What could be safer?"

"You never know," Mom muttered darkly.

I laughed at the time. I didn't have any idea, then, just how right she was.

❂

Miss Pearl Plummer was a thin little lady with a very sweet face and a very bad memory.

"This is one of Miss Plummer's hazy days, dear," Mabel the supervisor said. "She gets a little bit confused sometimes."

A little bit confused! That was the understatement of the year. Miss Plummer was nice, but a bit of a headache, until you got used to her.

When we met, she leaned so close to me that I could smell the faint scent of her face powder, and told me that this was her friend Ruby's house. Ruby had invited her to stay for as long as she liked, she said. I saw Mabel making faces at me, so I didn't say anything.

Then Miss Plummer's forehead wrinkled. "Where is Ruby?" she asked Mabel sharply. "There's something I have to do for her. And it's just slipped my mind."

Mabel smiled. "Ruby passed away, Miss Plummer," she said gently. "Last year. You remember."

A shiver ran down my spine.

The old lady stood perfectly still. Her face wrinkled even more. "Oh, yes," she said finally. "Ruby's gone. I'd forgotten." She looked very sad.

"Do you have any little jobs for Liz to do today?" asked Mabel, still in that gentle voice.

"Jobs?" Miss Plummer looked lost.

My heart sank. This was terrible!

"Where's your list, Miss Plummer?" Mabel asked. "Oh, dear. You've put it away safely, have you? Well, let's find it."

So my first job for Miss Plummer was finding the list where she'd written down my first job! Mabel whispered that she was always putting things away in "safe" places. So safe, sometimes, that they were never seen again!

This time we were lucky. The search took only ten minutes. But when we did find the list (carefully tucked away with Miss Plummer's clean nighties), all it said, in funny, spidery writing was: "Liz Free. 1 pkt hairnets (white, fine)."

"Well, there we are!" exclaimed Mabel, as if we'd discovered treasure. "Now Liz can run and get those for you, can't she?"

Miss Plummer looked pleased, and patted her hair. Then she glanced anxiously at me. "You'll be back soon, won't you, dear?" she asked. "I think Ruby has invited Elmo for dinner. And Alfie Bigge. And my hair's a fright!"

I nodded, dumbfounded. Mabel quickly waved to Miss Plummer and ushered me out the door.

"Don't worry, dear," she said comfortably as we went down in the elevator. "Miss Plummer has good days and bad days. Poor darling — she was very ill after her friend Ruby died. And now — well, she lives a lot in the past. But you'll be fine."

I wasn't so sure. The elevator stopped at the ground floor and we stepped out and went to Mabel's office.

"Why does she think this is Ruby's house?" I asked as Mabel opened a drawer and took out some money.

"Because it was," she said simply. "Golden Pines was Ruby Golden's home all her life. Her father built it. The whole street was named for it. The family owned a lot of land in Raven Hill in the old days. Including the Glen, next door, of course. You know they're going to build on it soon? Shame, isn't it?"

I nodded ruefully.

"Miss Golden would have hated it," tutted Mabel. "She loved the Glen. When Miss Plummer read in the *Pen* about it being built on, she was so upset! Still . . ." she sighed. "Everything changes. And no one can have their way forever. Not even Ruby Golden."

She shook her head, smiling. "Mind you, she'd never have agreed with that when she was alive. She was a very grand lady, you know, till the end. And always dressed the part. Marvelous clothes, makeup, jewelery, gallons of violet perfume . . . a real character."

"She must have been very rich," I murmured.

"Very," said Mabel dryly. "And very determined. She had this house turned into a retirement home about ten years ago. She and Pearl went on living here, but it was open to others, too. She wanted Raven Hill people to have a local place to come to if they needed care as they got older."

She handed me some money. "This will pay for the hairnets," she said. "Just bring back the receipt and the change."

I went to the door. Then my curiosity got the better of me and I turned back. "She talked about 'Elmo,'" I ventured. "Was that Elmo Zimmer? The *old* editor of the *Pen*?"

"Oh, yes," Mabel said. "He was a great friend of Miss Plummer and Miss Golden. There was a little gang of four, actually. Ruby, Pearl, Elmo, and Alfie. They were kids together, and stayed friends all their lives. Alfie was Alfred Bigge — you know the law office up at the end of Golden Road? That was Alfie's. He died over a year ago now, too. But his son carries on the business."

"I work for Elmo Zimmer's son," I said.

Mabel laughed. "Sadly, you won't get many points with Miss Plummer for that," she said. "Miss Golden didn't think much of Elmo's son. Nor of Alfie's. And whatever Miss Golden thought, Miss Plummer thought, too."

I left Golden Pines and walked up to the shops thoughtfully. It was strange to think of those four old people as kids, hanging out in the Glen just like we did. I tried to imagine Sunny and Nick and Tom and Richelle and me sixty or seventy years from now, and failed. I couldn't even start to think how it would feel to be old.

4

Day one

The following Thursday morning at five o'clock sharp, we were waiting outside the *Pen* office door. All of us had made it, even Richelle, who was there in body, at least, if not in mind. She stood in the doorway swaying slightly. Her eyes kept fluttering closed. I hoped Mr. Zimmer wouldn't notice.

Nick hadn't complained about the early start as much as I'd expected. I think he really had thought Help-for-Hire Inc. would be stuck with babysitting and dog walking. Nick wasn't the best with little kids. They made him nervous. They didn't have enough respect, and did disgusting and embarrassing things like wetting their pants and upchucking in public places. I don't think he had anything against dogs, really. But they often did embarrassing things in public, too, and Nick cared a lot about his image.

At two minutes past five, Elmo Zimmer appeared at the corner of the street. Elmo the third, I should say. Mr. Zimmer's son. He grinned shyly as he walked toward us. He did look like his father. Red curly hair, a round face, nice eyes. But his eyes, I thought, were brighter than Mr. Zimmer's. And his chin was more determined. You get the feeling that he wouldn't let himself be bullied by someone like Miss Moss, if he was boss of the *Pen*.

"Not this door! Use the back entrance," he called to us, beckoning.

We nudged Richelle awake, and Elmo led us around the corner to an alley that ran along the back of the *Pen* building. A roller shutter had been pulled up to show a big, echoing loading dock.

Mr. Zimmer was there, wearing shorts and a T-shirt with a penguin on the chest. When he saw us, his face broke into a relieved smile. "Ah, there you are!" he called. "So you *were* around the front! What were you doing there?"

The others groaned at Sunny and me.

"I bet Dad didn't tell you about the back entrance, did he?" said Elmo, loudly enough so the others could hear. I shook my head, smiling gratefully at him. He smiled back. He seemed much more — sort of — confident here, than he did at school. At school he was fairly quiet, and never said much. And he always disappeared as soon as classes were over. Never hung around talking or anything. So he didn't have any real friends. Well, none I'd ever noticed.

I introduced Nick, Tom, and Richelle to Mr. Zimmer. "Glad to have you on board," he said, shaking hands with them eagerly. His eyebrows had disappeared into his hair again. I saw Tom looking at him with interest. Any minute he'd be dragging out his pad and doing a sketch. Probably a funny one. Now is not the time, Tom, I warned him silently.

"Super! The wagons are loaded," said Mr. Zimmer. "Ready?"

Nick pulled the six route maps from his backpack. On Sunday, Sunny and I had worked out the route each one of us would take to cover the area. As Sunny had quickly pointed out, studying Mr. Zimmer's map, the way the other team had done, it meant a lot of walking up hills with the wagons full. We could do it more quickly by changing things around a little.

We'd taken the map to Nick's house. Nick had scanned it on his father's laser printer to make six copies. Tom had marked each copy with one of our names, and drawn in that person's route with thick red pen. Richelle had watched, and picked lint off her black jeans, which had gone through the wash with a tissue in the pocket. It was teamwork at its best, we thought. We were quite impressed with the result.

So was Mr. Zimmer. He beamed. "Very efficient," he said to Richelle. "You've planned it all beautifully." She shrugged and smiled serenely back at him. I exchanged glances with Sunny, who rolled her eyes.

We pulled our wagons out into the silent street. It was strange to see it so empty. No people or lines of traffic. Just an occasional car or bus speeding by, a lone jogger pounding along the pavement, and a ginger cat slinking home.

"Good luck," said Mr. Zimmer, as though he was sending us off to war. "Meet back here when you're finished, and I'll give you your pay. Ask Miss Moss to see you into my office." He held up a stern, plump finger. "And remember, a *Pen* to every home in Raven Hill. No exceptions."

We probably should have saluted, but as it was we just nodded and set off, Richelle, Elmo, and I one way; Tom, Nick, and Sunny the other.

The wagons were fairly heavy to pull. Mine had a squeak in one wheel. A sort of regular *gurgle-plop-squeak* that seemed very loud in the quiet street. I felt quite embarrassed by it, as if it was something wrong with me personally. As if my stomach was rumbling or something. Richelle's wagon, I noticed, was running perfectly.

To take my mind off the *gurgle-plop-squeak* I started talking to Elmo.

"Do you always help your dad on the paper?" I asked.

"Since early this year I have," he answered, his eyes on the ground in front of him. "He only started working on it himself then. He's a salesman, really. But he left his job and took over the *Pen* after my grandfather died."

His grandfather. Elmo Zimmer the first. Ruby, Alfie, and Pearl's friend.

"What was your grandfather like?" I asked curiously.

Elmo shrugged. "I thought he was great. A lot of people thought he was weird. He had this big white beard, and he yelled a lot. The *Pen* was his whole life."

He was silent for a moment, then went on. He seemed glad to talk. I got the feeling that he didn't get the chance very often.

"Granddad loved exposing rip-offs and things," he grinned. "He said only a local paper could help local people when they needed it. The paper never made him much money. But he didn't care. He didn't care about anything but news."

"He sounds great," I said sincerely.

Elmo smiled sadly. "He was. Even when he was dying, he was trying to tell us about some big story he had. He could hardly talk, but he was still muttering about it to Dad, wanting him to follow it up."

He glanced at me. "I know the office isn't much to look at," he said, flushing slightly. "Granddad never worried about things like that, and there's no money to fix things up yet." He tightened his lips and lifted his determined chin.

"Early this year, the office got broken into and all sorts of stuff get wrecked," he went on, looking straight ahead. "That's how Granddad died, really. The cops reckon he walked in on the vandals or thieves, or whoever they were. The shock gave him a stroke.

"And it turned out nothing was insured properly. So when Dad took over, he had to borrow a heap to buy all new computers and stuff. That's one of the reasons why we've got money troubles now. That and the *Star*." He trudged on, deep in thought.

Gurgle-plop-squeak went my wagon. I wished it would stop. Also, my arm was aching. And we hadn't even started yet.

"Did you print your granddad's big story?" I asked, to take his mind off his troubles.

Elmo grimaced. "We never found out what it was. No one at the office knew anything abut it. Not even Stephen Spiers. He's the senior reporter at the *Pen*. Not even Mossy." He grinned suddenly. "That's Miss Moss. Granddad always called her Mossy. Dad wouldn't dare."

The grin disappeared and he sighed, biting his lip. "Poor Dad," he mumbled.

I felt uncomfortable, and so sorry for him.

"Sheila Star stole someone else last Friday," he burst out. His mouth was set, and his determined chin stuck out. "Without notice again, too. It's driving Dad crazy."

"Who did she steal this time?"

"Felicity. Miss Moss's assistant."

23

The chewing-girl with the long fingernails. "She wouldn't have been much of a loss," I said disdainfully.

He laughed, in spite of himself. "You're right. She was pretty hopeless. All she had to do was type and answer the phone and take finished pages to the printer and stuff like that. And even that stressed her out."

He shrugged. "As it turned out, we were okay. We got someone better right away. But it could have been a real hassle."

We reached the corner where we were going to split up. Elmo stopped. "We've got to save the *Pen*," he said through gritted teeth. "We've got to."

I saw Richelle turn her head to stare at him curiously. She always thought it was odd when people cared a lot about things. Sometimes I'd try and explain it to her.

"It's like you care about clothes and stuff, Richelle," I'd say. But then she'd just look at me as if I was odd. That wasn't something she just *cared* about. It was life, to her, like breathing in and out. It couldn't be compared to anything else, in her opinion.

Elmo took a breath and looked straight at me. "The *Pen*'s been going for sixty years," he said. "And it's done a lot of good things. And whatever Miss Moss, or Terry Bigge, or anyone else says, there's no way Sheila Star's going to take it over and let it die. No way."

5

On the road

I thought about what Elmo had said as I started my rounds, carefully poking folded copies of the *Pen* through the bars of gates, or laying them on front paths. I felt proud to be helping. The work was easy. And I was earning money, too. Then I started to feel guilty. If the paper was so short of cash, maybe Mr. Zimmer couldn't really afford to pay us. Maybe we should be offering to work for nothing.

That was a depressing thought. I tried to put it out of my mind.

After about half an hour, my legs were aching and my right arm felt as if it was about to drop off. I changed hands yet again, and decided that it was quite fair to take money for the job. It wasn't as easy as I'd thought. I plodded on. I was getting a blister. *Gurgle-plop-squeak* went the wagon.

As I pushed the paper through the bars of the next gate, a toddler, with no clothes on except for a bib, staggered out of the open front door.

"Bee!" he squealed. "Bee-bee-bee."

Maybe "bee" was his word for hello. Maybe it was his word

for breakfast, because he headed straight for the paper in the gate, grabbed it, and started chewing it as though he was starving, drooling all over the headlines.

"No, no!" I whispered, trying to pull it out of his gummy little jaws. He opened his mouth, screwed up his eyes, and began to scream very, very loudly.

There were footsteps in the hall of the house. "Jason?" shrieked a voice.

I decided it was time to retreat. I let go of the paper and hobbled off down the street as fast as I could, my wagon *gurgle-plop-squeaking* in double-quick time behind me.

That was my first problem. It wasn't my last. It was getting later in the morning now, and people were waking up. People and animals.

In the next half hour, I was nearly bitten by two dogs and barked at by a Great Dane, which looked as if it could have swallowed me in one gulp. I was yelled at by a man who said I'd pushed the paper too far through the gate rails, so that it bent his rosebush. I was yelled at by another man who said I hadn't pushed the paper through the gate far enough, so it fell back onto the sidewalk.

I was yelled at by a woman who said I'd missed her house last week. I was yelled at by another woman who said the *Pen* was trash and she didn't want it. I stepped on a huge piece of bubble-gum that spread itself all over the sole of my shoe and stuck me to the pavement whenever I put my foot down. I put my hand on a banana slug in the paper slot below someone's letterbox. A little kid came and sat in my wagon and refused to get off. Then his mother shouted at me for letting him do it.

I trudged on and on. By the time I'd refilled my wagon from the bundle of *Pens* waiting at the pickup point, I was hot, limping, hassled, and exhausted. And I felt I was taking much too long.

At last, I turned into my own road, the last on my run. Sweat was pouring down my forehead by now. A couple of boys were walking toward me up the sidewalk. They were pulling wagons too, half-filled with copies of the *Star*. They must be part of the team that had deserted the *Pen*.

I looked straight ahead, trying to ignore them. My face was hot. I knew it must be red all over. My wagon squeaked and rattled. As soon as they were past, one of the boys muttered my name, then they both exploded into snorts of laughter. My face got even hotter.

I reached Golden Pines at the end of the road and stopped, panting, under one of the trees that hung over the sidewalk there. Below Golden Pines there was only the Glen, and the park. So now I could cross the road and start back up.

I looked at the big house set in its huge garden behind the ivy-covered wall. I didn't have to make a delivery here. Golden Pines needed a whole bundle of *Pens* to itself, so Mr. Zimmer brought its order when he was doing his car rounds delivering bundles to the stores and the hospital.

Miss Plummer would be getting ready for breakfast now, in her lovely bedroom overlooking the Glen and the park. She'd be smiling her sweet smile, looking forward to seeing Ruby, to ask her what she wanted to do. Or maybe this was one of her "good" days.

I looked at my watch. I couldn't rest here any longer. I had to get back to the *Pen* office. Cursing my wagon, my blister, and the bubblegum that was still sticking my foot to the pavement, I crossed the street and moved on.

○

"What are you doing back?" snorted Miss Moss as I peeped cautiously into the office. She put down the copy of the *Pen* she'd been reading.

"I've finished," I said. I edged inside.

She looked at me disbelievingly. "That's impossible. It's not even nine o'clock yet." Then she frowned. "Mr. Zimmer will have something to say if you've missed any houses," she warned. Then she glanced at the paper on the desk. "Mind you, this week it might be a blessing if you have."

I had no idea what she meant, so I didn't say anything,

She sniffed. "You can sit down now, and wait."

I sat down near the door on the long padded bench that ran down one side of the room. I felt like I was waiting for a doctor's appointment.

Miss Moss didn't say anything else. I watched her as she went on reading. She didn't look happy. Every now and then, she'd sigh heavily. The clock on the wall ticked. My feet throbbed in time with it.

After a while Miss Moss pulled a bottle and a rag from her desk and went over to the plastic palm tree I'd nearly stumbled into the week before. She started spraying its already shining green leaves, and polishing them with her rag.

"Would you like me to do that for you?" I asked. Maybe if I was helpful she'd decide to be less unfriendly.

"Certainly not," she snapped. Then she must have decided she'd been rude. Well, ruder than usual. "I prefer to look after this myself. It's mine," she explained. "Mr. Zimmer —" She paused, then raised her chin. "The first Mr. Zimmer, I mean, gave it to me when the plant I had turned up its toes. He said at least this wouldn't die. Or drop leaves." She looked fondly at the nasty thing, and went on polishing its sharp, stiff fronds.

The front door opened and a pretty, dark-haired girl came in. "Good morning, Miss Moss," she said. She glanced at me and smiled. I smiled back. This must be Felicity's replacement.

"Good morning, Tonia," said Miss Moss, barely looking at her.

Tonia went and sat in front of the computer at the other desk, put down her handbag, hung her jacket on the back of her chair, and began sorting out forms and cards. She certainly looked more efficient than Felicity.

I sat on the bench, waiting. The traffic was building up outside on the road, now. And still no one else had turned up.

Suddenly, I had an awful thought. I'd been so busy thinking about my own troubles that I hadn't thought about the others. But the more I did think about them, Nick and Richelle, anyway, the more worried I got. What if the others had just given up? What if they'd just abandoned their wagons and *Pens* and gone home?

Mr. Zimmer will be furious if all the Pens don't get delivered, I thought, working myself into a silent lather. *He'll put something in the paper about how unreliable Help-for-Hire is, and we'll never work again!*

6

Trouble brewing

The clock ticked. Sunny wouldn't just go home, I argued with myself. And neither would Tom. Tom wouldn't stop halfway. He'd finish the job and then complain about it afterward. He was a joker, but he wasn't irresponsible.

Was he? I squirmed. Miss Moss looked at her watch.

And just at that moment, the door opened and Sunny, Tom, and Nick walked in together. I jumped up. I'd never been so happy to see them in my life.

"How'd it go?" called Tom.

"Quiet, please!" snapped Miss Moss. She looked at him severely, and he ducked his head in mock dismay.

"How'd it go?" he breathed, mouthing the words with exaggerated care.

"I'm dead," I whispered. "What about you?"

He rolled his eyes to show the whites and let his tongue hang out the side of his mouth.

Nick groaned.

Sunny giggled. "It wasn't so bad," she said. "Good exercise."

We all groaned.

"Have you seen Richelle?" I asked.

They all shook their heads. "Elmo's around the back," said Tom helpfully.

Five out of six. But where was Richelle? We looked at one another.

"Maybe we'd better go and look for her," said Sunny. "She might have found the walk a bit of a problem."

"A bit of a problem! You don't say?" sniffed Nick. "If you ask me, Richelle's at home in bed right now."

There was a flurry of toots from the road outside. A car had stopped outside the *Pen* door, holding up the traffic. "Thanks a lot!" sang Richelle's voice.

Miss Moss raised her head. We looked at one another again. The car door slammed and the car drove off with a screech of tires. Richelle drifted into the office, cool, sleek, unruffled. Not a limp, or a drop of sweat, or a hair out of place.

"Hi," she smiled happily around.

Miss Moss's grim face relaxed slightly. "Good morning," she said.

Richelle came and sat down with us. "What was all that about?" I whispered. "Where's your wagon?"

"Around the back. Sam dropped it off for me."

"*Sam?*" Who's Sam?"

Richelle opened up her big blue eyes. "Oh, he's a friend of my sister's. He saw me sitting on a bus seat, and picked me up. I had a blister starting, you see?" She showed us a tiny red-rubbed mark on the inside of her foot. "So I couldn't walk anymore, could I?"

"Oh, of course not," drawled Tom. "If you had, you might have ended up with wall-to-wall blisters, like me."

31

She nodded, unconcerned. "I was quite hot, too," she confided. "And a woman looked at me in a funny way while I was delivering her paper."

"No!" Tom looked around, his eyes popping wide with pretend shock.

"Yes," said Richelle. "So Sam helped me deliver the rest of the papers. He said it would be best not to just leave them there. Then we went to McDonald's for breakfast, because I hadn't had time to have anything to eat, and I was starving. And then he brought me back here."

Nick lay back and closed his eyes. "I don't believe it," he muttered. "And I suppose he's going to do the same next week, is he?"

"Yes," said Richelle. "He said it was fun. And we'll try a new place for breakfast every week." She looked around at us, and smiled. "It's a good idea," she said earnestly. "The car makes the deliveries much quicker."

"Oh, Richelle," wailed Sunny. "How do you *do* it?"

"What?" said Richelle. And the frustrating thing was, she really didn't know.

○

A few minutes before nine, Mr. Zimmer came out of the inner office. He looked at us lined up on the bench. Tom was sketching, Nick was dozing, Sunny and I were talking, Richelle was filing her nails. He gave us a wobbly smile.

"All done, I gather," he said. "In record time, too. Good work!"

Miss Moss sniffed.

"Anyone called yet, Miss Moss?" Mr. Zimmer asked.

"Not yet," she droned. "But they will," she added ominously. "They will."

As if her words had been some sort of prophecy, the clock hands slid to nine o'clock, and the phone shrilled. Mr. Zimmer jumped. "Come into my office," he gabbled, beckoning to us.

As we went, we could hear Miss Moss coping with the caller. "Yes," she was saying. "We've just become aware . . . most unfortunate . . . printing error . . . yes . . . I'm sorry, madam, but . . ."

Tonia's phone rang and she answered it. "Good morning, *Pen* newspaper," she said. "Oh, yes, sir. Well . . . oh, I am sorry to hear . . ."

Mr. Zimmer put his hands over his eyes and his ears at the same time. "Oh, here we go," he moaned.

He bustled us through the door and into a dark, wood-paneled corridor. At the end of the corridor, we could see a big room filled with desks. That was where the reporters and editors sat, I imagined. But we didn't go down there. Instead, Mr. Zimmer opened another door to the left, and ushered us into a gloomy office lined with books and old wooden filing cabinets.

A huge desk cluttered with papers filled most of the floor space. On the wall behind the desk hung a portrait of a fierce-looking old man with curly hair and a white beard. Elmo Zimmer the first, I thought.

Mr. Zimmer opened a drawer and took out five envelopes. "I'm sorry I kept you," he began. "We've had . . . a few problems this morning. Now —"

The phone rang. He picked it up, listened, and sighed. "Oh,

yes, Miss Moss. No, that's all right. Put her on," he murmured. He squared his shoulders, waiting.

"Yes, Sheila? What can I do for you?" he said into the phone, in a harsh voice I'd never heard him use before. "I know about Stephen Spiers. He just told me. I hope he knows what he's doing, leaving the *Pen* for a rag like the *Star*." He winced, and held the phone away from his ear as the voice at the other end squawked loudly.

I jumped. Stephen Spiers was the *Pen*'s senior reporter, Elmo had said. Losing the delivery kids and that chewing-girl Felicity was one thing. Losing Stephen Spiers was another. No wonder Mr. Zimmer was upset.

"Thank you, Sheila," Mr. Zimmer said, still in that hard voice. "I'm aware of the errors. No. I don't know how they happened. Everything was checked as usual. Perhaps you have a friend at the printers' office, do you?"

He looked up quickly as the door opened, saw Elmo sidle in, and relaxed. He turned his attention back to the phone, which was squawking again. "Sheila. I have no intention of selling the *Pen* to you," he snapped. "I'd rather see it go bankrupt."

"You tell her, Dad," shouted Elmo. He looked angry and confused.

"Good-bye, then," said Mr. Zimmer firmly. He put down the phone.

I felt like cheering.

But Mr. Zimmer leaned his elbows on the desk and put his head in his hands. He didn't look like a man who'd just told off an enemy. Far from it.

7

Disaster!

There was a knock at the door. Mr. Zimmer looked up fearfully.

An immensely fat woman in a flowery dress swept in. Her face was streaked with tears and her sharp little nose was running. She was waving the latest *Pen*, open at the society pages. We had to shrink back against the office walls to make room for her.

"Zim!" she cried. "Oh, Zim, how could you do this to me? My pages are a catastrophe! I'll be a laughingstock!"

"Theresa, please!" begged Mr. Zimmer, glancing at us. "Just . . ."

"Every photograph wrongly labeled!" wailed the woman, ignoring him. "Look at this!" She pointed to a picture of a smiling bride and groom.

"'Little Poopsie carried off first prize as cutest pet in show,'" she read. "'Congratulations to proud owner Mr. Ralph Muldoon, eighty years young last week.' And look here! Under old Mr. Muldoon and his poodle you've put 'Glowing happiness for the bride and groom, who are planning a romantic honeymoon in

Hawaii.' Oh, how — how *appalling*! I'll never live this down. Never!" She began to cry again.

Mr. Zimmer looked helpless. Elmo stepped forward. "Mrs. Cakely, the whole paper's a mess," he said quietly. "Names spelled wrong. Sentences left out. Ads upside down. Pictures labeled stupidly. Mistakes everywhere. Someone's done it deliberately. To hurt the *Pen*."

Mrs. Cakely's sobs died down. She blew her nose, and looked reproachfully at Mr. Zimmer. "This is terrible," she announced, as though he wasn't all too obviously aware that it was. "And Stephen Spiers is leaving. After all these years. I can't believe it."

She raised her eyes to the portrait behind the desk. "Nothing like this *ever* happened in your father's day," she said.

Mr. Zimmer sighed.

The phone on his desk rang again. He picked it up and listened. "Yes, Miss Moss," he said finally. "Of course. Give me a minute, then send him in. And please ask Tonia to make coffee." He hung up and turned to Mrs. Cakely.

"You'll have to forgive me, Theresa," he said. "Terry Bigge is here, and I have to see him."

"Terry Bigge?" Mrs. Cakely's eyes sharpened and her curious nose twitched. "Old Alfie Bigge's son? Didn't he lend you the money to get the new computers and so on?" she asked. "What does he want?"

Mr. Zimmer looked away. "We have an appointment," he said.

Mrs. Cakely's nose twitched again. "Isn't he about to build on that land Ruby Golden left him?" she asked casually.

I pricked up my ears. She was talking about the Glen!

"I believe so, Theresa," murmured Mr. Zimmer. "Now, if you'll excuse me . . ."

"He'll make a fortune with that, won't he?" persisted Mrs. Cakely. "He's building luxury condominiums, so I hear. Luxury condos next to a park! My goodness, he'll make millions!"

She lowered her voice. "They say, of course, that Ruby was in love with his father, you know," she breathed. "I suppose that's why Terry got the land when she died. Good luck to him."

I exchanged glances with the others. Good luck for Terry Bigge. Bad luck for us.

Mrs. Cakely pursed her lips. "The building's going to cost a lot in the meantime, though." She paused, and finally got to the point. "Terry Bigge's going to need all the cash he can get, isn't he? Even the money he lent to the *Pen*?" She put her head to one side and regarded Mr. Zimmer. Like a bird waiting for a worm.

He smiled briefly and turned away. "If you go out the back, Theresa, Tonia will bring you some coffee. All right?"

Sniffing and wiping her nose, Mrs. Cakely allowed herself to be ushered out of the room by Elmo.

We all moved away from the walls and breathed out. Mr. Zimmer handed us our envelopes. "Thanks for your good work," he said, trying to grin. "See you same time next week, yes?"

"If there *is* a next week," muttered Nick as we filed out of the office. "This place is a rathouse. And even the rats are leaving."

Richelle was looking very put out. "How embarrassing!" she whispered. "Delivering a paper full of stupid mistakes. I hope no one saw me."

I caught sight of Tom's sketch pad. With a few quick, clever strokes of his pencil he'd drawn Mrs. Cakely, waving her arms, while Mr. Zimmer cowered behind his desk. I was feeling awful, and so sorry for Elmo and Mr. Zimmer, but I had to laugh, anyway. It was a very funny drawing. Tom flicked back a page and showed it to me. There was Miss Moss, polishing the leaves of her plastic tree. She looked crazy, and sour as a lemon. Everyone crowded around to look.

The door to the front office snapped open, and Miss Moss herself peered in at us. Tom whipped the pad around so the drawing was facedown against his chest, but he was too late. She'd seen it. We could tell by the way her eyes narrowed.

"Uh-oh," breathed Tom. I elbowed him in the ribs.

Now that the door was open, we could hear noises from the front office. Phones ringing, and angry voices. Some people had obviously decided to deliver their complaints personally. There was a shrill bark. That was probably Ralph Muldoon's poodle, Poopsie, objecting to being called his bride.

"You can go out the back way," said Miss Moss in an icy voice, glancing over her shoulder.

We obediently backed away, only too glad not to have to face her in front of an angry crowd. A tall man in a suit came through from the outer office. This must be Terry Bigge. I frowned as Miss Moss ushered him into Mr. Zimmer's room. How could he destroy the Glen just to make money?

"Zim!" we heard him call as he went in. "How . . . !"

The door shut, cutting off the rest of his words.

"Off you go, now," snapped Miss Moss, glaring at us. She went back into the front office and firmly shut that door, too. We were alone in the dark corridor.

"Psst!" the hiss nearly made us jump out of our skins. With

a creak, a door in the wood-paneled wall opened and Elmo's curly head peeped out. He beckoned. "In here," he breathed. "Quietly."

We crowded into the small, dark space. It was a storage room, full of brooms, mops, and buckets. It was built so cleverly into the wall that none of us had had any idea it was there.

"What . . . ?" began Richelle.

"Listen," hissed Elmo savagely. "Don't talk."

Richelle sighed, and fell silent. Even she wasn't going to argue with Elmo in this mood.

There were voices coming through the wall from Mr. Zimmer's office next door. Elmo put his ear to the paneling to hear more clearly, and Nick immediately did the same. Eavesdropping was second nature to Nick. He was the most curious person I knew, although Mrs. Cakely looked as if she'd come close. I sniffed. I disapproved of this snooping.

But when I heard Elmo's muffled gasp, and felt Nick's arm tense as he pressed his ear even harder against the wall, I changed my mind. I couldn't bear not to be in on the secret. And in a way, I reasoned guiltily, the more we knew about the *Pen's* problems, the easier it would be to help. I wasted no more time, but pressed my ear to the wall right alongside Nick.

". . . just a bit longer, Terry. A week or two at the most." It was Mr. Zimmer's voice. "Next week's issue has the Molevale Markets sale ads. Twelve pages of them. It's a huge boost for the *Pen*. I got the deal right out from under Sheila Star's nose. Do you know she had the gall to call this morning and offer to buy the *Pen* again?"

"What did you tell her?" asked the voice that must belong to Terry Bigge.

39

"What d'you think?" shouted Mr. Zimmer.

There was a moment's silence. Then his voice continued more softly. We had to strain to hear. "I know you think I'm crazy, Terry. But I can't let her have it. Not even for you. And look, it'll be all right. I can give you half the money as soon as Molevale Markets pay up. And the rest in a month. I promise you."

"What's happening?" whispered Tom, who was crushed back against the other wall, and couldn't hear a thing.

Elmo held up his hand warningly.

"Buddy, I . . ." Terry Bigge sounded uncomfortable. "You know the builders on this condo thing are really pushing me. I'll be in deep trouble if I don't give the go-ahead and pay up soon. You know I'd do anything for you, Zim, but . . ."

"Terry. Please!" Mr. Zimmer's voice broke in. He was pleading now. I shut my eyes. This must be very hard for him.

There was a long pause. I held my breath. I was sure Elmo was doing the same.

"All right," Mr. Bigge's voice suddenly boomed out strongly. "I'll try to stall them a bit longer."

Elmo punched his fists in the air in silent triumph. He beckoned to us in the dimness and we jostled our way out of the storage room. "Let's go!" Elmo hissed. "We've got to talk."

8

Terror in the Glen

We tiptoed down to the big room at the end of the corridor. Along both walls, separated with low partitions, were desks laden with ringing telephones, humming computers, and piles of papers. But no one was working at the computers, no one was reading the papers, and no one was answering the phones.

At the back of the room, around the coffeemaker, stood a group of people drinking from mugs and talking in low voices. Theresa Cakely was one of them. She was whispering behind her hand to the woman next to her, who was nodding sympathetically.

In one corner, a man with gray hair was packing belongings from his desk into a box. That must be Stephen Spiers, the deserter. He shot a look at Elmo, then quickly turned his head away.

Elmo led us out through another door into the place where we'd picked up the papers. The roller shutter that led out to the alley was closed now, and you could see that it had a cute little door in the middle of it through which staff could go in and out during the day. Our footsteps echoed on the cement floor.

Elmo turned to face us. "Sorry about that. But I wanted to make sure I caught you before you left, and I had to hear what was going on. Now, look, you won't ditch this job, will you?" he asked fiercely.

Nick grimaced. "Well, I don't know, Elmo . . ." he began.

"Of course we won't!" Sunny and I shouted together. It was so perfectly timed that we could have planned it. "Of course we won't," I repeated more quietly, looking straight into Nick's eyes, willing him to agree. He shrugged. We'll talk about this later, Liz, his black eyes warned.

"We'll probably have to stay on, anyway," Richelle remarked airily. "If we're going to go on with Help-for-Hire. I mean, we're not going to get any other jobs for a while, are we?"

"Why not?" I demanded.

"Well, because — you know — the phone number," said Richelle, eyeing me in surprise.

We all stared at her. She stared back.

"What do you mean, Richelle?" asked Sunny patiently.

"The number in our ad. There's only one, and it's been printed wrong," said Richelle. "Didn't you know? I saw it when I was at the bus stop. Sam and I rang the number from McDonald's. It's a laundromat. Well, they're not going to take messages for us, are they?"

"What?" exploded Nick. He slapped his forehead with his hand in frustration.

Tom and Sunny looked quizzically at Elmo. His round face turned pink.

"Let's get something to eat and go down to the Glen," I suggested quickly. "You come with us, Elmo."

"I can't go now," said Sunny. "I'm doing a tae kwon do morning class."

"*Sunny!*" I groaned. "Not again!"

"Are you training to be ruler of the universe or something, Sunny?" Tom complained.

But as it turned out he couldn't come, either, because he had to go home to watch his little brothers for a couple of hours. So in the end, we decided to meet at the Glen in the late afternoon instead. Elmo still said he'd come. I was glad. It would be good if he could forget the *Pen*'s troubles for a while.

✹

But when we finally did get to the Glen, far from forgetting the *Pen*'s problems, we talked about nothing else.

The Glen was lovely in the soft afternoon light. Birds were hopping around in the feathery bushes. Chipmunks scuttled around the rocks. Monty lay sleeping beside me. It was so peaceful. You wouldn't believe we were in the middle of the city.

We all felt it, especially Elmo, who hadn't been there for years. And so we started talking about how much we were going to miss the Glen when it was gone. And that meant we started talking about Terry Bigge and his condos. And *that* meant we started talking about the *Pen*.

"If Terry can wait for his money for just a couple of weeks, we'll be okay," said Elmo. "If he can stall the builders . . ."

"I don't see why he needs to build on the Glen at all," I interrupted. "He got it for free, didn't he? Why doesn't he just leave it alone?"

Nick looked at me disdainfully. "Because he's not a senti-mental idiot like you, Liz. He'll make a fortune out of the thing when it's done. You can't expect him to pass that up because of a few trees and possums."

"No," I scratched Monty's ears and frowned. I could see that it was too much to hope for, really. It wasn't the way most adults worked. And Terry Bigge obviously wasn't all bad. He'd lent Mr. Zimmer money when he needed it. And he was trying to hold off taking it back for as long as he could. I sighed.

"Couldn't your dad have gotten the money from a bank?" I asked Elmo.

He shrugged. "He didn't even try. See, Sheila Star tried to buy the *Pen* after Granddad died. Everyone thought Dad would sell. But we talked about it, and we both wanted the paper to stay in the family." His cheeks stained pink again. "I'd like to run it one day myself," he confessed, looking hard at a chipmunk scut-tling up a nearby tree.

Nick raised one eyebrow. You could see he was thinking Elmo was a bit of a nut case, too, wanting to take over a business like the *Pen*.

"Anyway —" Elmo saw his expression, but went on deter-minedly, "Terry wanted to help. He offered the money to tide Dad over. Dad thought he'd be able to pay the money back quite soon. But everything went wrong." He fell silent and sat brood-ing, his chin on his hand.

The light was fading now. The birds were silent. The Glen looked beautiful and mysterious. No one moved. No one wanted to break the spell and go home.

"Next issue will make money, your dad said," I offered, wanting to cheer Elmo up. "That's something, isn't it?"

"I guess so," he answered gloomily. "I just wish we had a good front-page story. We want Molevale Markets to get lots of people into their sale because of their ads. Then they might advertise every week. That'd help a lot. But for people to read the ads, they've got to open the paper in the first place. That means we need an exciting headline. And now with Stephen Spiers gone, that's going to be hard."

Everywhere you turned there seemed to be a problem. I shivered suddenly, and looked around. While Elmo had been talking, the Glen had grown very dim. The trees rustled, and there were scuttles in the shadowy undergrowth. Then out of nowhere an idea popped into my head.

"What about the big story your granddad was on to before he died?" I asked excitedly. "Couldn't you try to find . . . ?"

Elmo shook his head. "No chance. The office was completely cleaned up after the vandals got in, and nothing was found. What's more, Granddad's house was burgled just after he died, and everything was turned upside down there, too. We looked at every single paper before we filed it again." He looked down at his hands.

"No," he murmured. "We'll never know what the big story was now. It died with Granddad. And there's nothing anyone can do about it."

The leaves whispered. I shivered again. And then, without warning, Monty lifted his head and growled, and the hair on the back of his neck bristled under my fingers.

"What is it?" breathed Tom.

"I —" My voice stuck in my throat. Monty's growl became a whimper, and he pressed his head against my knee. I could feel him trembling.

Sunny sprang to her feet. "Who's there?" she demanded.

But there was no answer. There was utter stillness, as if the whole Glen was holding its breath. And then a cool, soft wind sighed through the trees, tumbling the leaves, swirling around us in chilly gusts, bringing with it a heavy, sweet scent of flowers. Monty threw up his head and howled.

And then we saw it. Something tall and pale was glimmering through the trees. It was moving. It was gliding toward us, its long white clothes fluttering. It made no sound. Not a stick cracked beneath its feet. Not a pebble shifted in its path. Not a leaf caught at its long white hair. It stretched out thin arms . . .

Richelle sprang to her feet. Her face was as pale as paper. "No!" she screamed. And then she was running. And we were running, too. Running away from the flickering white figure. Running through bushes and vines that caught at our clothes and feet and hair and tried to hold us back in the darkness. Running out of the Glen, and at last bursting thankfully into the brightly lit street, with its cars and houses and people. And safety.

9

Ghost story

"What was *that*?" gasped Elmo.

I licked my lips, stroking Monty's head, trying to calm him. "It was the ghost," I whispered. "The Glen Ghost."

"Don't be ridiculous, Liz!" snapped Sunny. "There's no such thing as ghosts."

"Well, what was it then?" demanded Tom. "It didn't make any noise. It floated. It was freezing. And —"

"And the dog," shuddered Richelle. "The dog — howled. It sounded awful." She made a disgusted face at Monty.

"Monty was scared," I said defensively.

"He wasn't alone," snapped Nick. His face was scratched and he was frowning furiously. "But it's crazy. Ghosts? I don't believe in ghosts."

"I do. Now," said Tom. He'd pulled out his pad and was sketching furiously. "I've got to get this down while I remember. We're eyewitnesses to a genuine haunting, for goodness' sake. We've got to tell someone."

"How about telling thousands of people?" said Elmo quietly.

We all turned to look at him. His lightly freckled face was still pale, but his eyes were sparkling.

"Well?" he demanded. "We were looking for a big local story, weren't we? So what are we waiting for? We've got to get back to the *Pen* and tell Dad. This is a story everyone will want to read. The Ghost of Raven Hill Glen!"

○

Mr. Zimmer was a bit worried about Elmo's ghost idea at first. But when he heard what the rest of us had to say, and saw Tom's drawing, he was convinced. Whatever we'd seen, the story was worth telling.

"Now, tell no one," he warned. "This has to be our scoop." His eyes sparkled, just as Elmo's had done. "We'll run rings around the *Star* this time," he said, and rubbed his hands. "This time *everyone* will read the *Pen*. And that means *everyone* will read the Molevale Markets ads. And Ken Molevale will think we're wonderful!"

I was pleased that the Glen Ghost was going to help Mr. Zimmer and the *Pen*. But I have to admit that I also had a sneaking hope that the ghost story might help the Glen, too.

"Maybe the city council will stop the Glen from being ruined now," I explained to the others. "Maybe they'll think it's worth preserving."

Cynical Nick snorted. "They preserve places that are historical, or sacred, or something. They don't preserve places that kids say are haunted," he jeered.

"You never know," I said. I paused. Good heavens, I was

48

sounding like my mother! Well, that couldn't be helped. I rushed on. "And you know what? I think that's what the ghost wants. I think it was Ruby Golden we saw. I don't think she wants the place where she used to play being destroyed."

"She shouldn't have left the Glen to Terry Bigge, then," said Richelle irritably. "And she should be haunting him now, instead of scaring us half to death."

"Don't talk silly, you two," snapped Sunny. "You know we couldn't really have seen a ghost."

"I think we did," I responded stubbornly. "And when Terry Bigge reads the *Pen* next week, I really hope he thinks so as well!"

○

For days after that, we were all in and out of the *Pen* office, helping Mr. Zimmer with the ghost story. He was keeping it really quiet. Only a few people in the office knew about it. At his suggestion, Tom redrew the sketch he'd done the evening we saw the ghost. It was very good by the time he finished, even Nick had to admit that, and Mr. Zimmer said that he was going to use it on the front page.

Tom pretended to be cool about this, but I could tell he was really excited. Actually, we all were. Our ad would be running again in this issue, too. For free, of course, since the phone number had been messed up last time. I expected we'd get lots of calls. After all, we'd be quite famous, with our names in the paper and everything.

On Tuesday, when I went to Golden Pines, Miss Plummer seemed to be having one of her "good" days. She had her list ready and waiting. So when I got back from the store with the apples and lemonade she'd wanted, I started to try to find out a bit more about Ruby Golden.

"You and Ruby used to play in the Glen when you were kids, didn't you?" I began.

She smiled and nodded, her faded blue eyes dreamy. "Ah, yes," she murmured. "Ruby and me, and Alfie and Elmo. We had great times."

"Do you think Ruby would have wanted the Glen to be destroyed, Miss Plummer?" I asked carefully. I didn't want to frighten her by talking about the ghost, of course.

She looked shocked. "Oh, no, dear. What could have put that idea into your head? The Glen will never be cleared. Ruby said so. She said it was to stay just as it is, forever."

Her soft forehead creased. She took hold of my hand and held it tightly. "Could you get Ruby for me, dear?" she whispered. "I need to talk to her."

I said nothing. I couldn't bear to upset her by reminding her that Ruby was dead, and Alfie and Elmo, too, or telling her what Alfie's son was going to do with his inheritance. So I changed the subject, and we chatted about other things till it was time for me to leave. I hadn't really gotten anywhere, I thought.

But at the Golden Pines gates, I looked next door at the bushes and trees of the Glen and shivered. And I realized that Miss Plummer's words had at least made me very sure of one thing.

Somehow, Ruby Golden's spirit really was watching over the place she'd loved so much. She knew it was in danger, and she was trying to protect it now in the only way she could. And she was using Help-for-Hire Inc. and her old friend Elmo's newspaper to do so.

○

Thursday morning finally came. We were all at the roller shutter on time — even Richelle, who came in style in her friend Sam's car. They were going to try breakfast at the Black Cat Café this time, she told us blithely. It was a trendy place, but Sam was paying, so that was okay. Great! I was so pleased for her!

With the others, I grabbed at the copies of the *Pen* lying in huge piles on the cement floor, and looked eagerly at the front page. **LOCAL KIDS SEE THE GLEN GHOST!** read the big black headline. And there was Tom's drawing, looking very spooky and realistic.

"It looks great, Mr. Zimmer," I said. I really meant it, too.

"Glad you're pleased," he laughed. "And look, forget all this Mr. Zimmer stuff. It makes me feel old. You'd better call me Zim like everyone else. Okay?"

We nodded. He looked very happy. And no wonder. Elmo had already told us that they'd checked every line of this issue when it arrived from the printing office. No mistakes this time.

Off we went, wheeling our wagons. I was pleased to find that I'd gotten a good one this time. Nick got the *gurgle-plop-squeak*, and he didn't like it, either. Serves him right, I thought. I still hadn't forgiven him for snickering at my idea about the Glen Ghost.

This morning, I seemed to fly around the streets. The route was easier the second time around.

Hurrying back up Golden Street I met the boys I'd seen before, delivering the *Star*. They'd obviously only just started their round, because their beautiful new wagons were still almost full.

I started to walk past them with my nose in the air. They laughed and sniggered again, but I didn't care. Didn't care, at least, until my eyes fell on the papers lying face up in their wagons. The *Star*'s big black headline read: **THE TRUTH ABOUT THE GLEN GHOST!** And underneath: **KIDS' TALE DOESN'T FOOL THE *STAR*.**

"Boo!" shouted one of the boys, wiggling his fingers at me. "Watch out for the ghosts, Lizzie!"

I almost ran away up the road, my ears and cheeks burning, my mind racing in circles. How on earth had the *Star* found out about our story? What had it written about us? And what was Mr. Zimmer going to say?

10

"How did this happen?"

Mr. Zimmer was *furious*. "How did this happen?" he thundered, throwing the *Star* down on his desk. "The printers only got the artwork for the front page last night. They had no time to tip off the *Star*. That means someone in this office is to blame. And I want to know who. Now!"

Everyone inside the small office fidgeted uncomfortably. The portrait of Elmo Zimmer the first glared down at us.

"Well, *I* didn't say anything, Zim," wailed Mitzi, the editor who'd worked on the story.

Zim's eyes, cold and hard for once, moved on to Miss Moss and Tonia, standing together by the door. Tonia caught her breath. She'd obviously never seen her boss in such a mood before. But Miss Moss lifted her chin and threw back her shoulders.

"Don't be ridiculous," she snapped. Her thin lips straightened into a rigid line. "I frankly don't understand why you are taking this tone with us, Mr. Zimmer," she went on. "The story has been known by six children for an entire week! Surely it's obvious where the leak came from."

"That's not fair!" exploded Elmo. "None of us told a soul.

Did we?" He appealed to us all, and we shook our heads vigorously. I caught sight of Richelle, who was looking highly insulted, and had a pang of doubt. But then I thought better of it. We'd all made sure she understood the importance of keeping quiet about the story. I didn't really think she'd told.

Zim sighed and turned away. His shoulder slumped. "Ah, what does it matter, anyway," he muttered. "It's happened." He opened a drawer and pulled out our pay envelopes. We took them from him silently, and followed Tonia, Mitzi, and Miss Moss out the door. Elmo was the last to leave. He joined us in the corridor, Zim's copy of the *Star* under his arm.

"Out the back," he muttered.

In the large back room, he spread the paper out on a table so we could all see it. I began to read, and as I did I felt my face get hot again. Just about all the things we'd told Zim were there. But because they were put into a different order, with bits of comment in between, they sounded silly.

And what was even worse, the *Star* reporter had gone and told Terry Bigge, as the owner of the Glen, what we'd been saying, and asked him for his opinion. He wasn't nasty, but what he said made us sound even sillier. Like little kids playing the fool.

He said he could quite understand why the local children, who liked to build forts and play hide and seek in the Glen, might make up stories like this to try to keep it from being developed. But business was business, and we'd understand that when we grew up. And all sorts of stuff like that.

We looked at one another in dismay. This made us look stupid. And it made the *Pen* look stupid, too, for reporting what we'd said.

"How embarrassing," said Richelle.

She'd never spoken a truer word. But there was worse to come.

At nine o'clock, the phones started ringing. More complaints. Some of them were about the *Pen* believing some kids' made-up ghost story. But more of them were from people who said they hadn't gotten their copies at all!

Zim called us into his office again. This time he was even angrier.

"You know the rules," he stuttered. "You deliver to every house in Raven Hill! But look here —" He ran a shaking finger down a list written in Miss Moss's spidery writing. "There've been complaints from 21 and 32 Windsor Street; 16, 18, and 24 Sweet Street; 19 Hodgson Avenue; 45, 48, and 51 Shirley Road; 7 and 11 Curnow Lane; 8, 12, 15, 23 Briller Avenue; 122, 157, 119, 67 Golden Road . . ." His voice droned on and on.

We stared, hypnotized, at the list in his hand. Finally, he broke off, tossing the paper to one side. We all tried to speak, but he held up his hand. "I don't want excuses!" he barked. "You just get copies of this list from Miss Moss and you go out and finish the job you've been paid for!"

"Zim — Mr. Zimmer, I delivered papers to all those houses on Briller Avenue," I quavered. "And Golden Road. That's my own street. I didn't miss a single house."

He shook his curly head. "I said no excuses," he snapped.

The phone on his desk rang. He snatched it up, still looking at us. "Molevale?" he said. "Yes, of course. Put him on." There was a slight pause, then: "Ken!" he exclaimed heartily. "How are you this morning? Seen the paper yet? Your ads look great!"

He listened, and as we watched, the fire died out of his eyes and a flush mounted in his cheeks. "Ah," he said. "Well, I'll . . . yes. Yes, Ken. Of course you would be. I'll look into it right away. Right."

He put the receiver down. "That was Ken Molevale of Molevale Markets," he said through tight lips. "He's just had a phone call to tell him that there are bundles of the *Pen* lying dumped in the Glen. He wants to know why he should pay for ads only the chipmunks can read. I want to know why I should pay to have my paper dumped. I could do that myself!"

"Mr. Zimmer," I began.

He turned his head away, but not before I saw his eyes, filled with hurt and despair. "Get out, will you?" he said. "Just get out."

Richelle went home after that. She'd had enough. But Sunny, Nick, Tom, and I stayed with Elmo. We huddled together in the back room, talking.

"None of us would have dumped papers, Elmo," I said to him. "You know that, don't you?"

He nodded. "I know it. But Dad doesn't."

"The point is," said Nick, leaning forward, his thin face intense, "how did the papers get there? And why did all those people call to say they hadn't gotten their copies? Sweet Street was one of mine. I did every house. I'm positive. And Liz thinks she did Golden Road properly, and Briller Avenue, and —"

"And I did Hodgson Avenue," broke in Sunny, wrinkling

her forehead. "And Curnow Lane. And Shirley Road. But I didn't miss any houses."

"Nor did I," added Tom. "It's weird." He began drawing big question marks all over his sketch pad.

I sighed. "I can't bear it," I wailed. "Everything was going so well!"

Elmo rubbed at his chin. "Let's go and get a copy of the list from Miss Moss," he said finally.

We trailed into the front office. Tonia looked up as we passed her and made a sympathetic face at me. But Miss Moss scowled.

"Miss Moss," began Elmo determinedly. "Could we —"

But at that moment, the front door swung open, and a broadly smiling woman in a bright blue suit swept into the room.

"Miss Moss! How are you today?" she cried in a ringing voice. She put down the black briefcase she'd been carrying, and her red lips stretched into an even wider grin.

Miss Moss drew herself up behind her desk. "Very well, thank you," she said tightly.

"Please tell Zim I'm here," smiled the woman. "I have something to show him." Her hard blue eyes darted around the room, taking in every detail, including the neat form of Tonia at the computer, and the group of us clustered beside Miss Moss. Her lip curled.

Reluctantly, Miss Moss picked up the phone and pressed a button. "Miss Star is here, Mr. Zimmer," she announced.

11

The enemy

So this was Sheila Star. The enemy. I stared at her. With her bright blue suit and her jangling gold bracelets, her puffy, waved blonde hair and her red, smiling mouth, she lit up the dim, dreary room like a flare. She looked confident, determined, and slick. My heart sank.

Miss Moss put down the phone. "Mr. Zimmer will see you here," she said coldly.

"That's fine by me!" laughed Sheila Star, glancing at us. "If he wants an audience, he can have it."

Zim walked into the front office with his head held high.

"What do you want, Sheila?" he asked. His voice was steady, but he looked tired and worn. The contrast between him and the bright, confident woman he was facing was very obvious. I felt Tom reaching for his pen.

The woman zipped open her briefcase and pulled out a couple of photographs. She handed them to Zim. We craned our necks to look. She saw us doing it, and her bracelets jangled as she patted her hair smugly.

"Unfortunately, your delivery team seems to have let you

down, Zim," she cooed. "One of our photographers happened to be by the Glen this morning, and took these snapshots. Isn't it awful?" She widened her blue eyes and pretended to look distressed.

Zim handed the photographs back without a word.

"I thought you'd better know," Sheila Star said, putting them carefully back into the briefcase.

"Thank you very much," said Zim grimly. "But you shouldn't have taken the trouble. I was aware of the situation."

"*Were* you?" Sheila Star's eyes widened again. She was the picture of innocence. I felt Nick stir behind me. I knew why. I was thinking the same thing.

"Yes. Ken Molevale called me. I guess it's you I have to thank for telling him about the dumping," Zim was saying.

The woman shrugged. "Well, the poor man had spent all that money," she trilled. "I really felt it was the —"

"The least you could do." Zim finished her sentence for her. "Yes. Well, thank you again, so much, for your trouble."

"I suppose Ken might feel he should refuse to pay for the ads, now," Sheila Star persisted. "What a shame, Zim. I know how you were depending on that money. I'm so sorry."

"I'm sure you are!" exclaimed Mr. Zimmer. He turned away.

But Sheila Star caught his arm and held him back. "Zim, it's time to be sensible," she breathed. "Stop playing around with this paper and all this" — she glanced at us — "all this silly, childish stuff. You know you aren't a newspaper man. Let me buy the *Pen*. Then all your troubles will be over."

Zim spun around to answer. But Elmo got in first.

"All our troubles would be over if you'd just leave us alone!"

he shouted, his voice breaking with fury. "*You* keep bribing our staff to leave! *Your* goons scrawled graffiti all over our building! *You* got some spy to change last week's *Pen* so it was full of stupid mistakes!"

Sheila Star opened her mouth to speak, but Elmo wasn't finished.

"*You* stole our lead story this week and made it look silly," he raged on. "*Your* delivery team followed ours this morning and stole people's *Pens*. And *you* had the copies dumped in the Glen, then got *your* photographer to take pictures. And *you* told Mr. Molevale that Dad had let him down, so he'd refuse to pay. Didn't you? *Didn't you?*"

Sheila Star raised her eyebrows. "Really, darling," she drawled to Zim. "Your son is rather overemotional this morning."

"Good-bye, Sheila," said Zim. He put his arm around the trembling Elmo's shoulders.

The woman smiled, and walked to the door. Then she turned, patting her briefcase. "I'm sure you understand, Zim, that I'll really have to publish this dumping story. It's my public duty, isn't it?"

She sighed while her blue eyes sparkled. "I'm sorry to expose such a respected old paper. I'd love to be able to follow my heart instead."

"You don't have a heart," said Zim.

An angry look flashed across her face. She threw open the door and flounced out, nearly bowling over Terry Bigge, who was trying to come in. She pushed by him without an apology and strode off.

Scowling, Terry walked into the office. "What was that woman doing here?" he asked immediately.

"Coming to crow," said Zim. "And threaten."

"She's a nasty piece of work," growled the other man. He fiddled with his dark blue tie. "Zim, I've just seen the *Pen* —" he looked at us almost guiltily. "A *Star* reporter called last week and said some kids were spreading crazy rumors about my land. So I just said a few things in reply. I wouldn't have said a word if I'd known you were running the story. I'm really sorry."

Zim looked at him gratefully. "It's okay, Terry," he muttered.

"It's not okay. That woman tricked me," Terry retorted.

"She did set up the dumping, Dad," cried Elmo passionately. "I know she did."

"Her delivery team was following us, too," I added. "I saw two of them. I didn't think about it at the time, but their wagons were much fuller than they should have been down the bottom of Golden Road. They must have had *Pens* under their copies of the *Star*. They'd been picking *Pens* up as fast as I delivered them."

"I think you're right," said Zim slowly. "I owe you all an apology." He bit his lip. "I'd be grateful if you'd each run out now and drop off some more copies for the people who've called in. I'll pay you extra for your time."

But none of us would take his money, of course. Even Nick. Sheila Star might have had no heart. But we did.

❁

It was hard to see how much worse things could get for Zim, Elmo, and the *Pen*. But that just goes to show, as Mom says, that you never know. A couple of days later disaster struck again, and in a way none of us could have expected.

It was Tuesday night, and I'd gone to a movie with Sunny. She had a free night from her endless classes, for a change.

We'd gotten off the bus on the main road and were walking home. It was dark, and there weren't many people around. We glanced at the *Pen* office as we always did when we went past, but it was dark and shut tight. Elmo and Mr. Zimmer quite often stayed late at the office. But not tonight, apparently.

We turned the corner and went on our way. But as we passed the alleyway where the *Pen* roller shutter was, I caught a glimpse of something out of the corner of my eye. Something that made me stop dead. A wavering flicker of light.

"Come on!" demanded Sunny impatiently.

"Sshh! There's something weird in the alley," I whispered. The skin on the back of my neck was crawling.

Sunny snorted in exasperation. "You're ridiculous, Liz Free! Can't you see? The little door in the roller shutter's ajar. It's moving in the wind and letting out the light from inside."

I breathed out in relief, because right away I could see she was right. No ghost, then. No restless spirit, guarding the *Pen* office. Just a light. And that meant Elmo and Zim were working late after all.

"Let's go in and say hi to Elmo," I suggested. "We could tell him we've had a great response to the ad already."

Sunny laughed. "If you call three babysitting jobs and two dog-walking jobs a great response."

But when I got to the door and pulled it open, I hesitated. The lights weren't actually on inside the loading dock at all. There was just a sort of gleam, coming from somewhere inside the building.

"Are we going in or not?" hissed Sunny, jostling me from behind.

I stepped through the door and onto the cement floor beyond. Sunny followed. Shadows flickered in the shafts of half-light that came from the back room doorway. We climbed up to it, and peeped in.

12

Help!

The big room where the *Pen* staff worked was completely empty. The only sign of life was a big flashlight that stood all by itself on one of the center tables, casting a beam of light against one wall. That was where the gleam in the loading dock had come from.

"They must be in Zim's office," I whispered. I turned back to Sunny. "Look, I think we should just forget about this and go. We might scare them, creeping up on them like this."

"Scare *them*?" Sunny looked up at me, grinning mischievously. "It's not *them* who's scared, if you ask me. Don't be such a wimp!"

With me trailing behind her, she darted into the corridor that led toward the front office.

"Sunny!" I breathed. But she wouldn't stop, and I had to follow.

Despite the light from the flashlight in the back room, it was dark in the corridor. Zim's office door was shut. Through it we could hear voices. In the dimness, I saw Sunny's teeth flash in a grin. She raised her hand to knock.

And then there was a bang inside the office, as if a box had been overturned, and a strange, rough voice swore. I gripped Sunny's arm. That wasn't Zim's voice. And it certainly wasn't Elmo's.

We began backing away, hardly daring to breathe. Who was it? Was the office being robbed? I was terrified. But that was nothing compared to how I felt when the office door clicked and began to open. Whoever was in there was coming out!

With a rapid twist, Sunny reached across me and pulled open the door to the tiny storage room where we'd hidden with Elmo. In my panic I'd completely forgotten it was there. We whipped inside and Sunny pulled the door shut behind us. I shrank back against the side wall. My heart was beating so hard I thought I was going to choke. The voices were louder now. And we could hear footsteps. There were two men. And they were coming closer.

". . . should be right," one voice said to the other, deep and low. ". . . no use . . . quick as we . . ." The door muffled the words my ears were straining to hear.

". . . might just as well . . . the old devil will . . . lucky . . . back . . . tinderbox . . ."

We heard the footsteps pass us and gradually fade as the intruders moved toward the back of the building.

"Stay where we are," whispered Sunny.

I nodded, though it was too dark for her to see me. I knew she was right. The men could have left. But they could just as easily be still hanging around.

We stood rigidly in our places while the minutes ticked by, not daring to move in case we made a noise. It was stuffy in the storage room now. And hot. I carefully shifted away from the wall a bit. My back was sweating where it had been pressed against the wood. And the wood itself was warm. Very warm.

I thought about that for a long moment. I can hardly believe now that it took me so long to work out what was happening. And when it did, I was so paralyzed with fright that I just stood there for a few seconds, clutching at Sunny's arm and not able to speak.

"What!" she hissed. "What is it?"

I finally found my voice. "Fire!" I gasped. "In Zim's office. We've got to get out!"

She looked at me wildly, then put out her hand to touch the wall. She snatched it back. "Hot!" she muttered. "Quickly!"

We wrestled the heavy door open and burst out into the corridor, careless now of who might hear us. Out there I could smell smoke. See it, too, oozing out in wisps from the crack under Zim's door. Maybe we could put out the fire! Without thinking, I darted up the corridor toward the door and reached for the handle.

"No!" shrieked Sunny, lunging for me. "It will spread the fire! Don't open it!"

Of course. I knew that. I'd heard it in fire safety lectures a million times. But in my panic I'd forgotten. Thank heavens for Sunny. I spun around, not knowing what to do next.

"The front door will be deadlocked," Sunny reasoned, gripping my arm. "We'll have to go out the way we came. Come on!"

We stumbled together toward the back of the office. We'll call the fire department from the back room, I was thinking. Then we'll get out. Then . . .

But Sunny was exclaiming in horror. And in a second, my ideas were tumbling into ruins. The back room was on fire, too.

And the flames were leaping and reaching for the ceiling, licking up the walls. The door to the loading dock, the roller shutter and safety, was completely blocked. Even as we watched, the fire started to roar. Papers on the wall began to catch fire and float around in the air. Smoke billowed out toward us. Sunny slammed the door.

"Back!" she ordered, and again we thundered up the corridor. It was hot and smoky now, and Zim's office door was patched with black as the fire inside raged.

We ran, coughing, into the front office. Sunny closed that door, too, and stuffed a cherry red jacket Tonia had left on the back of her chair into the crack underneath.

"Dial nine-one-one!" she shouted.

So I did, with shaking fingers and a stuttering voice, watching Sunny frantically searching Miss Moss's desk for keys that would open the deadlock that was holding us prisoners.

I hung up. "Soon as we can," the voice at the other end of the phone had said.

But would it be soon enough? I could hear the fire now. It had burned through Zim's door. It was roaring and raging in the corridor. Already Tonia's jacket was turning black. Soon, in a few minutes, the fire would break through to the front office. And we were trapped. My eyes began to sting with smoke, and with terrified tears.

But Sunny wasn't giving up. She grabbed an old metal wastepaper basket and jumped onto the visitor's bench.

"Cover your eyes," she called. And then she was throwing the basket straight and hard through the pretty old-fashioned window above the door, and colored glass was showering down to lie like little jewels on the murky-patterned carpet. She beckoned to me, and bent her shoulders.

"Climb up," she panted. "Get out. Watch the glass. Jump. Keep your knees bent."

"Sunny!" I sobbed. "What about you?"

"I can do it by myself." She glanced back at the door to the corridor. It was starting to blacken. "Hurry," she said through gritted teeth.

13

Escape

I climbed up on Sunny's shoulders, slipping and shaking, and scrambled for the window frame. There were only a few bits of glass left in it, and I plucked them out with my fingers and threw them down to the street. Then Sunny pushed herself upward and I pulled myself, arms straining, muscles feeling as though they were tearing apart, up through the open gap and out into the wonderful, free, fresh air of the night street.

I half fell, half jumped out onto the path. Somewhere I could hear fire engines. They were coming. But the fire was roaring!

"Sunny!" I screamed, staggering to my feet. "Sunny, come on!"

There was a bang against the door, and a scramble, and then a little face appeared in the hole where the window had been. Two dark eyes, a determined chin, a fringe of silky black hair. Then there was a pair of shoulders, and a twisting body. And then Sunny was jumping lightly down beside me, grinning as though this was some ordinary gymnastics lesson and she was the teacher's pet.

Well, I can tell you, I vowed that moment that I'd never

tease Sunny about her gymnastics again. Or tae kwon do. Or anything else. She could take up weightlifting and mountain climbing combined, as far as I was concerned.

We turned to look at the *Pen* building. Smoke was billowing through the empty window frame now, and we could hear roaring and crackling from inside. We backed away, gripping each other's hands, as the scream of the fire engine sirens came closer. All we could do now was wait.

I was shivering, although the night was warm. I thought about Zim and Elmo, at home watching TV or reading or something. They'd heard the fire engines. But they wouldn't know it was their business that was burning. They wouldn't know that terrible sound of alarm was for the *Pen*.

❋

The rest of that night was like a blur. I can't remember a lot of it properly. I remember Mom coming to get me, and her face as she came running up to me and grabbed me in her arms. I remember her talking to Sunny's mother, and putting her hands on Sunny's cheek, then hugging her tight.

I remember the street, wet with water from the firefighters' hoses as we walked to the car. I remember Zim and Elmo arriving and standing watching the whole thing, not saying anything, just staring, their faces pale under the streetlight.

Mom must have taken me home, then, and put me to bed, because the next thing I knew I was waking up in the daylight and thinking I'd had some sort of dream.

Then I noticed how my arms ached, and felt my sore ankle,

and the bump on my head where I'd hurt myself jumping from the window. I saw that it was ten o'clock. Ten o'clock! And then I just lay in bed for a while, while things slowly came back to me.

The whole gang had called while I was asleep, and at lunchtime we met in the Glen. Sunny and I were heroes, of course. Even Richelle roused herself to give us a hug and say how glad she was we were safe.

The others were full of questions — especially Nick, of course. But we really couldn't tell them a lot.

They finally gave up on us and said they'd wait for Elmo, who would be sure to make more sense. But when Elmo did come, he was so silent and sort of hurt-looking, that I think even Nick found it hard to question him. For a while, anyway. But Nick's curiosity always got the better of his sympathy in the end. And so it did this time.

"How bad is it?" he asked.

Elmo hunched his shoulders. "Dad's office is a write-off," he mumbled. "And the back room's completely burned. But because Liz and Sunny raised the alarm so quickly, the rest is pretty good really. Well . . ." he grimaced. "It's black and wet and smells disgusting. But it can be cleaned up. Dad and Tonia and Miss Moss are working on that now. I can't stay long. I'll have to go back and help." He stared at the ground. It was obvious that he didn't want to talk. But Nick persisted.

"Have they found out how the fire started?" he demanded.

Elmo frowned. "Gasoline and rags," he said. "In the back room and in Dad's office. That's why it flared up so fast. And the building's old. Old paneling. Lots of paper lying around. All that."

He fell silent again. Then he looked up. The freckles on his cheeks and nose stood out against his pale skin. "The door in the roller shutter was forced. But the police think someone who knew the building well was involved."

He took a deep, shuddering breath. "I think they think Dad did it," he whispered.

"That's not sensible," protested Richelle. "Why on Earth would someone burn down his own place?"

"Because he's got money troubles," muttered Elmo. "If the building burned down, Dad'd be able to get the insurance money, see, and then . . ." his voice died. His mouth quivered, and he bit at his lip.

Tom and Nick looked away hastily, and Richelle glanced down at her jeans and began brushing at them. They didn't want to see Elmo cry. But I was too astonished to be embarrassed. I grabbed at his arm.

"But that's crazy!" I exclaimed. "Sunny and I know Zim's voice! We would have recognized it." Sunny nodded vigorously.

"The trouble is . . ." Elmo swallowed and went on. "You only heard a few words."

"I'd still know Zim's voice if I heard it," I said stubbornly. I jumped to my feet, and winced at the jab of pain from my sore ankle. "We all know who lit the fire. It was Sheila Star. Or, at least, some men Sheila Star hired. I'm going to call up the police and tell them!"

"Hang on, Free," drawled Nick. "Don't just rush off and start jabbering to the cops and accusing people. They'll just think you're a silly kid being loyal to her boss, or something. We have to get some evidence. Then they'll have to listen to you."

I stared at him. It was irritating, but I could see he was right. I dropped back down on the ground.

"Sheila Star's got a spy in the *Pen* office," said Elmo, clenching his fists. "It's obvious. All the mistakes in the issue before last. And the leaking of the ghost story this week. And now the fire." He pressed his lips together angrily.

Looking at Elmo's angry face, I realized he was right. But who was it?

14

The spy

"Think," Tom urged Sunny and me. He sat cross-legged with his sketch pad on his knee, drawing question marks. "What did you actually hear while you were in the storage room? Maybe there's a clue there."

"I only heard a few words," I said slowly. "One voice saying, 'Should be right . . . no use . . . quick as we . . .' and then the other saying, 'might just as well . . . the old devil will . . . lucky . . . back . . . tinderbox.'"

Tom had been scribbling the words on his pad. Richelle leaned over to look. "That doesn't make any sense," she commented. But Nick's eyes were sparkling.

"Yes, it does!" he exclaimed. "You just have to fill in the gaps. The first man was probably saying Zim's office would burn all right, and that it was no use hanging around and they should get out as quick as they could. And the next one was maybe saying they might just as well do the job properly or the old devil wouldn't pay them, and it was lucky they had enough gasoline to light a fire in the back room as well. And that then the building would burn like a tinderbox."

"That's very clever of you, you know, Nick," commented Richelle.

Nick looked smug. Praise from Richelle was rare indeed.

Tom frowned. "But who's the old devil?" he asked.

"Sheila Star, of course," said Nick impatiently.

Tom shook his head. He flipped back the pages of his pad and considered his sketch of Sheila Star. "No," he said finally. "She's glamorous looking. I don't think they'd call her an old devil."

Nick irritably flicked a stick away from him. He didn't like his theory being interfered with. But I agreed with Tom. The phrase didn't fit Sheila Star. Then the thought struck me. Maybe it did fit somebody else . . .

"Oh, look," said Richelle, looking at Tom's picture. "When did you do that?"

He shrugged. "She came into the office last Thursday."

Richelle nodded distractedly and went on looking at the sketch. I remembered that she hadn't been in the office when Sheila Star came in. She pointed with a long, smooth finger.

"You've got the collar of her shirt wrong," she said critically. "The knot was much looser than that."

"No, it wasn't!" Tom looked cross. He wasn't used to having his works of art criticized.

"Yes, it was," said Richelle calmly. She yawned and stretched. "Anyway . . ." she caught sight of a chip on her nail polish and began inspecting it.

"Richelle —" She didn't look up as I spoke, and I touched her hand.

"Mmm?" she murmured.

75

"Richelle," I persisted, giving her hand a little shake. "How do you know what her shirt looked like?"

"Oh, Liz, what does it *matter?*" drawled Richelle. But I didn't let go of her hand, and she sighed. "I saw her when I was having breakfast with Sam, didn't I?" she said.

"Are you sure?"

"Of course I am," snapped Richelle. "She came in with Tonia while . . ."

"*What?!*" Elmo and the others sat bolt upright and goggled at her.

"What's up?" Richelle inquired. "You know Sam and I went to the Black Cat Café for breakfast. I told you. We had croissants and hot chocolate. It was very nice. We were in a booth in the back, and Tonia and this woman, whoever she is, came in and had a coffee."

"Richelle!" I squeaked.

She stared at me, wide-eyed. "What's the matter? I've got a right to have breakfast, haven't I?" she demanded.

Elmo jumped to his feet. "Of course you have!" he shouted. His face was red now, instead of white. His eyes sparkled fiercely. Richelle shrank slightly away from him. She probably thought he was crazy.

"Richelle, you're amazing!" exploded Nick. "Don't you understand?" He tapped Tom's sketch. "That's Sheila Star. And Tonia isn't supposed to even *know* her, let alone be talking to her in a coffee shop."

"Oh," said Richelle blankly. "Well, that's strange."

"It sure is," Elmo growled. "And we're going back to the *Pen* office right now. Tonia's got a bit of explaining to do."

❂

But as it happened, Tonia didn't explain anything much. When the cold, angry Zim, backed by Miss Moss, confronted her with Richelle's story, she just raised her eyebrows and half-smiled.

"Oh, all right," she said calmly. "I work for Sheila. Why else do you think she'd have hired a dork like that Felicity girl? Only so you'd need to take me on in her place."

"Get out!" spat Zim.

Tonia picked up her neat, leather handbag, sitting incongruously on the blackened visitors' bench. "It'll be a pleasure," she sneered. "If you think I like spending my time in this hole, you're wrong. Even for double pay and the chance to have some fun with the computers it was a pain. No wonder you can only get kids and an old sourpuss to work for you."

"You . . ." Miss Moss was speechless with rage.

Tonia smiled nastily, and started for the door. On her way, she flicked a finger at Miss Moss's plastic palm tree, which had miraculously escaped total destruction. "Good-bye," she said to it. "You're the liveliest thing I've had to look at for two weeks."

"You can expect a call from the police," Zim shouted after her. "Don't think you're going to get off that lightly. Spying is one thing. Arson is a criminal affair."

Tonia spun around. Now her face was shocked and angry. "What are you *talking* about?" she spat.

"I'm talking about you passing on information about this building so that Sheila's goons could get in and put a torch to it. That's what!" yelled Zim.

Tonia pointed a shaking finger at him. "Don't you dare say things like that!" she shrieked. "You can't pin that fire on Sheila and me. Everyone knows you tried to burn this place down yourself." She glared at him, panting. Then she whipped around again, and disappeared out the door. They heard her feet clicking on the sidewalk as she walked rapidly away.

Miss Moss and Zim looked at each other.

"I'll call the police station now, Mr. Zimmer," said Miss Moss grimly. "Will you meet the police here?"

I opened my mouth to say something, but then closed it again. I didn't have any proof of what I'd been about to say. Only a feeling that there was something wrong here.

Tonia had admitted being a spy for Sheila Star. She had put mistakes into the *Pen* final pages by changing them after hours, before she took them to the printing office. And she had shown Sheila our ghost story. But when I thought about her shocked eyes as she spun around to face Zim just now, I couldn't believe she'd helped with the fire.

But if she hadn't, who had?

15

The end of the line?

I tried to explain how I felt to the others, while we were helping clean up the loading dock. Zim had gotten permission from the fire department to set up a temporary office there.

The police hadn't laid any charges against Zim yet. They had listened to what he said about Tonia, he said, and were concentrating on her for a while. By mid-afternoon, he wasn't thinking about proving his innocence anymore. All he cared about was getting the next day's *Pen* out on time.

"The *Pen*'s never missed an issue, and it's not going to start now," he said, running his hands through his curly hair. "Is it, Elmo?" Elmo shook his head, his eyes as determined as his father's.

"But I don't see how it's possible!" whimpered Mitzi the editor, who'd been called in to help. She looked around at the smoke-blackened loading dock with dismay.

"We have rented computers, and there is a temporary phone line in," Miss Moss told her crisply. She, of course, was well organized already. Her desk was tidy, her rented computer in place.

The plastic palm, only slightly melted, towered behind her like something from a monster movie.

"There should be no real difficulty," she went on. "The printers got most of the pages yesterday afternoon, fortunately. They only need the front section now. And they say they'll work all night if necessary."

Zim bit his lip. "It's good of them. I owe them plenty. But they never said a word about money when I called. Just said they'd do whatever they could to help."

"So they should!" exclaimed Miss Moss. "The *Pen* has been their best customer for more than sixty years! Loyalty must surely count for something."

Zim looked at her gratefully. "It does with me, anyway," he said. You could see he was talking about her, as well as about the printers.

Miss Moss's cheeks colored slightly, and her grim mouth softened, as though she was about to say something. But then she tossed her head and turned away. Displays of emotion were not suitable for the office, in Miss Moss's opinion.

Zim, Mitzi, and some of the others started redoing the front pages. Zim had some story about drains he thought was pretty good. I couldn't get very enthusiastic about it myself, but I guess there's no pleasing everyone. We went back to our clean-up. And I tried to convince the others that my theory about Tonia was right.

"The errors, and the leaking of the ghost story and everything — well, they were just troublemaking for the *Pen*," I said. "Like stealing the staff, and the graffiti. But the fire — that was different. Sheila Star's horrible. But would she go as far as that? And the fire just doesn't sound like something Tonia would get involved with."

"Maybe she just left the door open, not knowing what Sheila Star had planned," said Nick.

The others nodded.

"I don't think . . ." I began.

Richelle tossed her head impatiently, and threw aside her broom. "I don't know why you always want to make things so *complicated*, Liz," she complained. "It's boring. I'm going out to get a drink. Anyone coming?"

Tom hadn't eaten for at least forty minutes, so of course he had to go with Richelle to get something before he fainted. Nick went, too. He said he was hungry, but really he was just sick of working.

"Listen, Elmo," I said when Sunny and I were alone with him. "I've been thinking . . ."

"Oh, be careful, Liz," he interrupted, straight-faced. "You don't want to hurt yourself."

Sunny gave a surprised snort of laughter. I realized that none of us had ever heard Elmo even try to make a joke before.

"No, listen," I persisted. "You know how Sunny and I heard the men say 'old devil will' — well, what if it didn't mean what we thought it meant?"

"What do you mean?" asked Elmo with interest.

"What if what they really said was 'old devil's will'?" I paused dramatically. "What if they were talking about your granddad's will? What if it's got some sort of damaging evidence about them in it? What if his will is hidden somewhere in the *Pen* office, and they wanted to find it, or destroy it?"

Elmo took a breath to answer, but suddenly another thought struck me.

"The vandals that got in, the night your grandfather had his stroke!" I exclaimed. "What if they weren't just making a mess, but actually looking for the will?"

My thoughts were racing now. "That might be why your granddad's house was robbed as well after he died," I went on. "These people, whoever they are, looked for the will in his house, and in this office, and finally, they tried to burn this place down to get rid of it once and for all!"

I looked from Elmo to Sunny, my eyes shining. "Well?" I demanded. "Well, what do you think? It all fits, doesn't it?"

Elmo smiled slightly. "Well, yes. It all fits," he admitted. "But unfortunately, Liz, there's a major problem. Granddad's will wasn't lost."

This only stopped me for a minute. "He might have made a new will," I persisted. "New wills always take the place of old wills. That's the law. The new will might have been the one that was hidden."

But Elmo shook his head. "There was no funny business about Granddad's will. His lawyer had one copy, and another copy was in the safe in his house."

He thought for a moment. "And even if there had been something odd," he added, "why would it matter to anyone else but us?"

"That big story he was talking to your dad about just before he died, maybe," I whispered. "He might have put the details in his will! Or even *with* his will! In the same envelope, or something."

Sunny sighed. "I hate to say it, Liz," she remarked, with her head to one side. "But sometimes I think Richelle is right. You *do* like to make things complicated."

I looked across the room to where Zim, Mitzi, Miss Moss, and a couple of people I hadn't met were slaving away over their hot, rented computers. "I just wanted to help," I mumbled.

"The best way you can do that," said Sunny, putting a bucket and mop into my hands, "is to get moving with the clean-up."

So I went back to work, rubbing at my sore ankle and feeling sorry for myself. Of course, I should have been concentrating on feeling sorry for Zim. But I didn't know what was about to happen, did I?

○

At about five o'clock, the bomb dropped. The phone rang, and Zim took the call. No one took much notice at first. Then gradually we heard his voice rise. We all looked around to where he was standing at his desk. His cheeks were flushed. His eyes were startled.

"But I can't believe you'd do this, Terry!" he was saying. "Don't you know what happened here last night?" He listened for a long moment. Then suddenly, his mouth dropped and his shoulders slumped. It was as though all the fight had been knocked out of him.

"Yes," he said dully. "Yes, I see." He glanced at his watch. "The banks are closed. I can't do anything now. It's too late. If only you'd called . . ." He listened again. "Yes," he said finally. "I understand, old buddy. No, don't worry. We've given it our best shot. I'll see you in the morning."

He put the receiver down gently and sat quite still for a moment, his eyes vacant.

Elmo ran over to him. "What's happened?" he asked fearfully.

"That was Terry Bigge," murmured Zim. "The builders and the bank are forcing his hand. The fire was the last straw. They know he's got the right to take over the *Pen* if I don't pay him what I owe. They've told him that now I clearly can't pay and if he doesn't take over the paper by nine o'clock tomorrow, they'll ruin him."

"But . . ." Elmo was white.

"He's been arguing with them all day, but they won't budge," Zim droned on. "He's run out of time. And so have we." He put his face in his hands. "I'm sorry, Elmo," he said in a choked voice. "I'm sorry."

16

Surprises

There was a terrible silence in the big, echoing loading dock. Then Miss Moss spoke.

"I never liked that Terry Bigge," she growled. "As Mr. Zimmer always said — the first Mr. Zimmer, I mean — he isn't half the man his father was."

"I don't suppose you think I am, either, Miss Moss." Zim gave a half-smile. "But at least I've tried. And so has he."

He turned to look at his worried staff and tried to speak cheerily. "And, look, if all goes well, we'll pull out of this yet. Terry will own the *Pen*, but I'll go on running it. And one day, I'll get the funds to buy it back. You wait and see."

Elmo fidgeted, and glanced over to us. I had the feeling that we should go. He and his father probably wanted to be on their own.

We muttered our good-byes and left through the roller shutter. My ankle was throbbing and my head ached. But I didn't want to go home. I was furiously angry.

"That Terry Bigge!" I hissed. "All he thinks about is money."

"That's unfair, Liz. He hasn't got any choice," said Tom reasonably.

"Zim shouldn't have borrowed money from him in the first place," Sunny put in. "It's not good to borrow from friends. Zim should have gone to the bank and done the thing properly."

"Oh, well . . ." I sighed. "It's no good wishing after the event."

"I think a bank would still give Zim a loan, you know," said Nick after a moment. "The *Pen*'s had its problems, but it's a good old business."

"But the transfer's got to happen at nine tomorrow!" I exclaimed in frustration. "Zim hasn't got *time* to see a bank manager now, Nick! Oh, if only Terry could get sick and not turn up for the meeting!"

"That's a good idea," said Richelle approvingly. "Let's do that, then."

"What?" I stared at her. She stared back, smiling.

"You're suggesting," I snarled, "that we go and hit Terry Bigge on the head, or spit in his coffee so he gets a disease, or something?"

She rolled her eyes. "You really are ridiculous sometimes, Liz," she sighed. "I'm not saying anything like that. I'm saying we should just go and ask him to *pretend* he's sick."

"He won't do that!" said Sunny scornfully.

"Why not?" asked Richelle. "It's what I always do when I don't want to go somewhere. He probably just hasn't thought about it. But if we ask him to do it — very nicely — he'll probably say yes." She nodded, as though that settled the matter, and turned her attention to brushing a speck of ash from the edge of her skirt hem.

After a moment, she looked up. We were still gaping at her. "Well?" she demanded. "Are we going, or not?"

○

Terry Bigge's office was up some stairs in a small group of shops at the top end of Golden Road.

We walked as fast as we could, but my ankle really was sore and it wasn't till after five-thirty that we found ourselves staring at the glass door with BIGGE AND BIGGE ATTORNEYS lettered on it in silver. Hanging in the center of the door was a CLOSED sign.

"Rats!" exclaimed Tom.

But Nick coolly reached out and pushed at the glass door. It swung open under his fingers.

"Nick!" I exclaimed. "We can't just . . ."

"We can. This is an emergency!" he whispered.

We tiptoed up the stairs. At the top, there was an elegant apricot-pink reception area, with a shining white desk and two visitors' chairs. A few closed doors were strung out along a short hallway on either side. We hesitated. What should we do now?

The high-pitched laugh from behind the closest door took us by surprise. I clutched Tom's arm instinctively. I felt a bit silly at first, till I saw that he'd grabbed Sunny's. Then there was a rumble of a man's voice. Terry had a client with him!

We looked at one another and with one movement backed away behind the white desk. Suddenly, I think, we'd all started to have second thoughts. Maybe Terry wouldn't be too happy about a bunch of soot-covered kids sneaking up his stairs after hours.

The door opened. We ducked down behind the desk. Tom had to fold his long legs up like one of those collapsible rulers before he could fit. I could feel Sunny beginning to quiver. *Don't giggle, Sunny!* I thought at her sternly. *Don't you dare!*

"Well, darling, I'll see you tomorrow," trilled a familiar woman's voice. "And, Terry, I can't thank you enough!"

My eyes widened. Sheila Star! What was she doing here?

"Your thanks are appreciated, Sheila," laughed Terry Bigge. "But your check will be even more so. Just don't forget to bring it with you."

"Of course I won't!" Sheila Star's high heels jabbed into the carpet right in front of the reception desk. I held my breath. If they saw us . . .

But they were much too interested in each other to look around them. Their feet passed the desk and moved out of sight, toward the exit door.

"I'll let myself out, Terry," Sheila Star said. She sighed happily. "Hasn't it been a long haul?" she said. "But I knew I'd get the *Pen* in the end, if I caused poor little Zim enough trouble."

"You'd never have gotten it without me," Terry Bigge reminded her. "And don't you forget it. He'd never have sold to you, no matter how bad things got. It was just lucky he was fool enough to take that loan when I offered it."

"Poor man," tittered Sheila Star. "He'll explode when he finds out you're selling me his precious paper on the very day he signs it over to you. I feel almost sorry for him."

"Well, don't," snapped Terry Bigge. "He deserves everything he gets. He was an idiot to sign that agreement with me. He could have easily gotten a loan from the bank on much better terms."

"He thinks you're his friend, darling," remarked Sheila Star dryly. "And as trustworthy as he is."

Bigge laughed. "Like I said. He's a fool! Like his father. And mine, for that matter."

We hunched, frozen, under the desk while they said their good-byes. Then we saw Terry's feet pace briskly past us and back into his office. As quietly as mice, we got to our feet and began to move toward the exit.

We could hear the man moving around in his office, packing up to go home. His door hung wide open. It seemed impossible that the five of us could escape unnoticed. But luckily, Terry Bigge was a man who liked luxury, even at the office. The pale carpet was thick, and the heavy door well-oiled and silent. In less than a minute, we were on the street and running (well, in my case, limping as fast as I could!) back to the *Pen*.

17

Elmo's plan

"I can't *believe* this!" Zim's eyes were nearly popping out of his head.

"I can!" snapped Miss Moss. "I never trusted that man. Never! A smart young swindler. That's what Mr. Zimmer used to call him. The first Mr. Zimmer, I mean. If he said to me once, he said a thousand times, 'Alfie's my best friend, Mossy, and I hate to say it,' he used to say, 'but that boy of his is no good.' And now you see?" she nodded fiercely. "He's been proved right."

Zim ran his hands through his hair. "I really believed in Terry," he said simply. "I really thought he was lending me the money because our dads were such good friends. I never thought twice about signing the agreement."

He screwed up his face and punched at his forehead. "Fool!" he muttered savagely. "I've been such a *fool!*"

"Never mind about that now, Mr. Zimmer," ordered Miss Moss. "Now we have to *do* something! We *cannot* let Sheila Star take over this paper." She rounded on us sharply. "Is that agreed?" she barked.

We all jumped like rabbits and nodded.

"But what can we do?" asked Zim helplessly.

"We will simply have to get the money to pay off that — that villain," said Miss Moss, and closed her lips, as though that was her final word on the subject.

"I agree," cried poor Zim. "And how do you suggest we achieve that? By nine o'clock tomorrow morning?"

There was silence. Then Elmo spoke. "I know," he said. He lifted up his chin as we all stared at him in surprise. "Tomorrow morning, instead of giving the *Pen* away for free," he said, "we sell it."

"We can't do that, Elmo," said Zim gently. "The *Pen*'s always been free. No one cares enough about it to want to buy it."

"If they know it's in trouble, they might," insisted Elmo. "If we go around Raven Hill tonight with notices saying the *Pen* needs help because of the vandalism, and the fire —"

"Elmo, please! I know you're trying to help, but this won't work," groaned Zim. "It won't, will it, Miss Moss? You tell him."

Miss Moss frowned and pursed her lips. Then she surprised us all. "I think it's an excellent idea!" she pronounced. "And I think we should start producing the notices your son suggests as soon as possible."

She went and sat down at her computer. "What should I say?" she demanded, looking straight at Elmo.

"Head it, 'Save the *Pen!*'" he said without hesitation. "And then say, 'The *Pen*, Raven Hill's local newspaper for more than sixty years, is threatened with closure . . .'"

Miss Moss typed like lightning. Elmo went on dictating, pacing up and down behind Miss Moss's chair.

When the notice was finished, Miss Moss took it over to the

Rapid-Print shop across the road. She caught it just as it was about to close and bullied the assistant into staying to print out multiple copies.

"They will be ready in one hour," she said when she returned. "I suggest these children call their parents to tell them where they are, and then get something to eat. After that, we can begin delivery."

"Then," said Zim, "I will go back to helping Mitzi produce the *Pen*. If we're going to charge for it, we'd better have a front page, don't you think?"

He went off whistling. I couldn't help thinking that despite everything he was enjoying Miss Moss and Elmo's great plan as much as they were.

I called home quite happily. But my mother wasn't happy at all.

"Absolutely not, Elizabeth!" she said, her voice high and indignant over the phone. "After last night? No way! You come home this instant!"

"Mo-o-m!" I pleaded. But it was useless. The only stay in execution I got was that I was allowed to have a burger with the others, then collect some pamphlets for delivery on our own street, before I came home.

○

I trudged down Golden Road in the dark, slipping leaflets under doors, still furious and embarrassed. The gang had felt sorry for me for having to go home. Sunny's mother, after all, had laughed and simply asked her daughter if she had a jacket! I felt like such an overprotected dork.

Still, I had to admit I was tired. My knees were shaking with weariness. By the time I finally reached Golden Pines, I'd almost started to be grateful to Mom for being such a worrywart.

I pulled out a whole bundle of pamphlets from my bag and went inside the big old house. The vast hallway, with its lift and winding staircase, was deserted in the yellow lamplight.

Then Mabel came hurrying out of her managerial office. She looked rather distracted, and stared when she saw me. "Oh, Liz!" she exclaimed. "Miss Plummer isn't with you, is she?"

"No," I said confused. "Is something wrong?"

"We've lost Miss Plummer," Mabel said unhappily. "When we went to get her for dinner, she wasn't in her room. Now I find out that no one's seen her since her afternoon nap. Inexcusable! She must be out on the streets somewhere. I've had to call the police."

"Why would she have left?" I asked.

Mabel frowned. "I'm afraid that silly *Pen* story about the Glen Ghost upset her, Liz," she said. "She's been hazy ever since she read it. Talking nonstop about Ruby. And now she's taken off to look for her, I suppose. Dear, oh, dear."

Her phone rang and she whisked off, leaving me alone in the hall feeling guilty. I hadn't thought about Miss Plummer reading the *Pen*. But of course she would. Mabel had told me that on her "good" days she read a lot.

A thought struck me. "She wouldn't have gone into the Glen, would she, Mabel?" I called. But Mabel was busy talking on the phone, and just shook her head and waggled her fingers at me.

I looked at my watch. I had about ten minutes before I was due home, and about twenty minutes before Mom would start to worry. I slipped out of Golden Pines and headed for the Glen.

18

Lost and found

The night was absolutely still. In the Glen, the trees and bushes clustered together thick, dark, and wild on either side of me as I felt my way along the rough, rocky track we always used. I wasn't really scared. *Not really,* I thought. Ahead was the clearing where the gang always sat.

"Miss Plummer?" I called softly.

There was no answer. I tried again. "Miss Plummer! Pearl! Are you there?"

There was a faint, stirring noise. The whisper of a voice. The drifting sound of a breeze running through the leaves. A cold, cold breath of air. Shivering, my heart beating wildly, I strained my eyes to see into the blackness.

"Pearl?" I called again, and stepped into the clearing.

And as my foot hit the ground, a pale figure stood up and held out its thin arms to me. My nose was filled with a faint, sweet, flower scent I remembered. My eyes began to water. My breath ached in my chest.

"I'm here," quavered the figure. "Ruby's gone, but I'm here. I had to come. I had to do something for Ruby. I knew I'd remember what it was, if I came here. And now I do remember. The envelope's quite safe. In the tree that never dies. Elmo is so clever. Everything will be all right now. But just now, I'd like to go home."

Then Miss Pearl Plummer was tottering toward me, and I was running toward her and putting my arms around her small, cold shoulders. And then, together, we were walking out of the Glen.

○

We caused a sensation when we turned up in Golden Pines. Miss Plummer, despite her tiredness and confusion, was pleased by the warm welcome. She smiled very graciously, and murmured greetings and thanks all around.

But Mabel didn't let anyone fuss too much. Within a few minutes, the old lady was wrapped in a blanket and whisked upstairs to a warm bed and a cup of soup.

"And a visit from the doctor," Mabel said when she came down, "though I really think she's fine."

She gave me a quick hug. "I can't thank you enough, dear," she said. "We did look in the Glen, you know. I can't think how we missed seeing her. She does sometimes go down there, look-ing for Ruby, if she's hazy. We don't say much about it, of course. Don't want to give other people ideas."

She gave me an amused, sideways look. "So now you know the secret of the Glen Ghost," she said dryly. "I couldn't help laughing when I read the *Pen* story. Imagine little Miss Plummer giving six grown teenagers such a fright."

"I —" I bit my lip, and thought better of what I was going to say. Because I couldn't afford a long discussion. I had things to do that couldn't wait, and I was going to have to work hard on Mom and Dad before they'd agree to cooperate.

❂

In the end, Mom actually drove me back to the *Pen* office. Since I was obviously intent on self-destruction, she said, she may as well help me — and do some shopping as well. Molevale Markets was open on Wednesday nights, and their sale was still on.

So it wasn't long before I was pushing through the door in the roller shutter and facing the surprised looks of Zim and Miss Moss.

"We're finished, Liz," called Zim. "Mitzi's taken the last pages to the printers. And the others are still out with the leaflets."

"It's not that," I said. I clasped my hands. It had all seemed so clear down at the Glen. But now I wasn't so sure. And besides, Miss Moss was here. I'd really hoped she'd be off delivering pamphlets with the gang.

"What's up?" inquired Zim.

There was a bang from the back door and Nick stepped into the loading dock, followed by Sunny, Elmo, Richelle, and Tom, all looking very pleased with themselves.

"You can't have finished yet," protested Miss Moss. "You can't possibly have delivered hundreds and hundreds of —"

Nick spread out his hands. "You underestimate Help-for-Hire," he grinned. "We have contacts!"

"A lot of kids at the gym took bundles to deliver on their way

97

home," explained Sunny. "The basketball team took some, too. The flower committee at Saint James was meeting in the church hall. They took a bundle each. That skateboard gang took a lot. There was a parent-teacher event at the school. They took bundles. Molevale Markets are giving one to every customer tonight —"

"Are they?" Zim looked surprised and touched.

"Yes. And most important," grinned Tom, "the hot dog man outside the station is, too."

"Why are you here, Liz?" asked Richelle. "I thought your mother wouldn't let you stay?"

Nick looked at me properly for the first time. His nose twitched. "Something's up," he said. "What is it, Liz?"

So everyone was looking at me then, and I had to get over my nervousness and tell. About Miss Plummer, and what she'd said to me in the Glen.

". . . The envelope's quite safe. In the tree that never dies. Elmo is so clever," I finished.

The faces around me were blank. I turned my head and looked at Miss Moss. I could tell that she at least knew exactly what I meant.

"What do you think?" I asked her.

She nodded briskly. "I think it's worth a try," she said. She spun around in her chair and dragged the drooping plastic palm from behind her desk into the middle of the floor. Then she squatted down beside it and began pulling out the brown curly stuff that filled its pot.

"Mossy — Miss Moss — what are you doing?" exclaimed Zim in horror. It was like sacrilege, seeing Miss Moss treating her precious palm that way.

"If this isn't a tree that never dies, what is?" she grunted, tearing out handfuls of brown stuff and throwing it to the floor in a growing pile. The tree's leaves trembled as she worked, and one fell off. But she took no notice.

Then she froze, one hand deep in the pot. A strange expression crossed her face. We all watched, fascinated, as she slowly pulled her hand out. Clutched between two fingers was a fat envelope.

She got up, dusting her hands, and passed the envelope to Zim. He took it, his face alive with curiosity. Then, as we all crowded around, he opened the envelope, pulled out the wad of papers inside, and began to read aloud.

After the first few lines, we were clutching one another in amazement. After the first page, Zim had to sit down.

"Miss Moss," he croaked. "Call the printers. Tell them to stop the presses. If the *Pen*'s going, it's going with a bang, not a whimper. We're going to do a new front page."

"Yes, sir!" cried Miss Moss. And for the first time since I'd known her, she was beaming all over her face.

19

Zim tells a story

Terry Bigge was in bright and early on Thursday morning. He stepped cautiously through the door in the roller shutter and found Zim alone at his desk in the loading dock.

Zim looked up without a smile.

Terry Bigge grimaced. "I've brought the papers for you to sign, Zim," he said, putting his head down and pressing his lips together as though he was very upset. "I'm sorry, buddy. I just don't have any choice."

"You do, you know," said Zim coldly.

"Now, Zim, don't give me a hard time," warned Terry Bigge in a slightly harder voice.

"I've only just begun, my friend." Zim folded his hands and leaned across the desk. "I want to tell you a story," he said.

Terry's eyes narrowed.

"A long time ago," began Zim dreamily, "there were four friends: Elmo Zimmer, Alfie Bigge, Ruby Golden, and Pearl Plummer. As kids they used to play together in the Glen, the patch of forest beside Ruby's house."

"Look," snapped Terry. "I don't know what this is all about, but I haven't got time to sit here fooling around, Zim. I've got a meeting at the bank."

"You can wait for this," said Zim. "It won't take long. When the four friends grew up, they all ended up staying in Raven Hill. Elmo Zimmer started the *Pen*. Alfie Bigge became a local lawyer. Pearl Plummer made hats in a shop up Golden Road. And Ruby Golden — well, she was very rich, and she devoted herself to charity work and having a good time.

"They got older. Ruby fixed up her will with Alfie Bigge, who of course she used as her lawyer. She'd already made Golden Pines into a nursing home and given it and most of her money to her church. Now she only had the Glen to leave.

"She left it to Alfie, her favorite. If he died before her, the Glen would go to his son, in his place. That was you, Terry."

Terry Bigge's mouth was set in a hard line, but his fingers were trembling as he raised them to smooth his glossy hair. "Have you . . . ?" he began. But Zim held up his hand.

"No, I haven't finished yet," he said coldly. "As it happened, Alfie did die first. And the Glen was yours. Or was it?"

"Of course it was, Zimmer!" snarled Terry, all pretense of friendliness dropping away. "The old girl's will was perfectly clear on that."

"Oh, yes," smiled Zim, tapping the desk with steady fingers. "The first will, made ten years ago. But what about the second will, Terry?"

Terry Bigge's face turned an ugly, dark red.

"Ruby Golden went to see you after Alfie died, didn't she,

Terry?" said Zim. "She was a suspicious old bird. She knew Alfie would never have destroyed the Glen. But she wasn't so sure about you anymore." He smiled briefly.

"So she asked you to write her a new will, in which the Glen was left to the people of Raven Hill, on condition that it was kept in its natural woodsy state for everyone to enjoy."

"What a lot of nonsense!" Terry spat. "You're making up a fairy tale to stall me. Well, it won't work, Zimmer! You haven't got a shred of proof for any of this."

"We'll get to that in a minute," said Zim calmly. "I'm nearly finished. You tried to talk Ruby out of making the new will, didn't you? But she insisted. She waited while you had it typed up, and signed it then and there. Then she went home to Golden Pines, leaving the will with you for safekeeping, as she'd always done with your father.

"But she felt uneasy, Terry. You shouldn't have tried to talk her out of the new will. You made a big mistake there. She didn't trust you. So the next day, she made another will, just like the one you'd just done for her. And she wrote a letter saying why. She put the will and the letter in an envelope and hid it away.

"When she knew she was dying, she got the envelope out and gave it to her friend Pearl. She asked her to pass it on to Elmo Zimmer. She knew he would deal with it. She died in peace, believing that she'd taken care of everything. As she always had."

"This is fantasy, Zimmer!" sneered Terry Bigge. "You're just . . ."

Zim raised his voice. "The trouble was, Pearl Plummer was so grieved by her friend's death that she got very ill. In fact, she nearly died, too. When she got better, she'd become very forgetful.

"She didn't remember the envelope she'd put away safely on the night of Ruby's death. All she knew was that there was something that Ruby had wanted her to do. So she fretted, without knowing why. And of course, in the meantime, you'd quietly destroyed the later will, and had produced the old one. The one that left the Glen to you."

"How dare you!" Terry Bigge roared. "You're . . ."

"Be quiet!" snapped Zim. "Just listen. I want you to hear every word! When Pearl read in the *Pen* that the Glen was going to be built on, she called Dad. She was really upset. I remember him telling me about it. But he didn't tell me what came later. He went to see her. He took her out for a walk in the Glen. And there, suddenly, she remembered. She remembered about Ruby, and you, and the new will.

"They found the envelope where she'd hidden it — in a hat-box in her room. And Dad read the will, and the letter that went with it." Zim stared coldly at the other man's white face.

"He'd never thought much of you, Terry," he said. "But that afternoon he found out how bad you really are. Like I did, last night, when I read them, too. And his note besides." He slowly drew the bulky envelope from the drawer of his desk.

Terry Bigge sprang to his feet. "Where did you get that?" he shrieked. He snatched at the envelope, but Zim pulled it away.

"Oh, no," he said coldly. "This is for the police, not for you. You had your chance, Terry. Dad felt he owed your father that, didn't he? He didn't tell you where he got the will, because he didn't want you worrying Pearl, but he said he wouldn't turn you in if you did what Ruby had wanted, and gave the Glen back to the people.

"He said he'd keep the will and Ruby's note here in the *Pen* office in safety for a few days. He said he'd write a note of his own to put with it. Then he sent you off, and later he told Pearl what he'd done, and where he'd hidden the envelope. He told her everything was going to be all right.

"But you couldn't bear to do the right thing, could you? You decided you had to have the money the Glen would bring you. You couldn't give that up. And you thought no one knew about the will except Dad. Without it, it'd only be his word against yours. So that night you brought your goons in here and you wrecked the place looking for it. You couldn't find it. Dad had hidden it too well. But it cost him his life. Because he came back to the office while you were still here, didn't he?"

Terry Bigge stared at him, white-faced. His forehead was gleaming with sweat.

"Did one of your bullies hit him, Terry?" shouted Zim, suddenly losing control. "Is that what brought on the stroke that killed him?"

20

The big story

"No!" Terry shouted. "No! He – he fell. He came in on us suddenly. He started yelling, the silly old fool. Then he just fell. I never touched him!"

"You may as well have killed him with your bare hands." There were tears in Zim's eyes now. "By the time he was found and taken to the hospital, he had no hope. 'Big . . .' he kept muttering to me. 'Big . . . story.'"

Terry groaned.

Zim almost smiled through his tears, and shook his head. "I thought he was being a newspaper man to his last breath. But he wasn't, was he? He was trying to get me to follow up your story, Terry. The Bigge story. The story of a man who'd sell out anyone and anything for money."

"Zim!" Terry Bigge licked his lips. He glanced right and left like a hunted animal.

"Zim, we're talking about millions, here! Millions! I'll – I'll share it with you. We can be partners. You can keep the *Pen*, and have all the money you want to run it. Think about it! Even without your debt to me, you're in deep trouble, thanks to the fire and Sheila Star. I'll be surprised if you'll be able to pay the printers' bills. And they won't support you forever, Zim."

Then he had an inspiration. "Think about Elmo," he urged. "He's a bright boy. He deserves a chance. Do you want him to believe his father's a feeble failure all his life?"

Zim looked at him with something like pity. "Whatever Elmo thinks about me," he said steadily, "at least he knows I'm not a liar, a cheat, and a thief. He knows I wouldn't betray a fine old lady who trusted me. He knows I wouldn't pretend to be a man's friend so I could sell him out. He knows I wouldn't risk burning down a whole street of buildings to destroy evidence against me. He knows I wouldn't leave an old man lying helpless and dying. I'm just glad you haven't got any kids. I'd feel sorry for them." He sighed as he watched the panting man in front of him.

"And it was all for nothing, wasn't it, Terry? Because our story about the Glen Ghost stirred dear old Pearl Plummer's memory all over again. And last night she remembered just enough about what Dad had done with the will to help me find it. And, Terry, I'm not going to destroy it like you would have done. I'm going to hand it straight to the police."

With a growling cry, Terry Bigge lunged at him across the desk, grabbing him around the throat. "You fool!" he hissed through gritted teeth. "You fool, Zimmer. Now I'm going to have to —"

"That's enough!" The deep voice echoed around the loading dock. Then the men in uniforms were jumping down from the blackened back office where they'd been hidden with us. And they were tearing the choking hands from Zim's neck. And then, while Elmo and Miss Moss and all the rest of us rushed to Zim's side, Terry Bigge was handcuffed, screaming, struggling, and swearing, and taken out into the street and into the waiting police car.

The car had only just sped away, and we had barely caught our breath, when Sheila Star stepped brightly through the shutter. She glanced at the policeman standing guard, smiled, catlike, at Zim, then looked around.

"Oh, dear, more trouble?" she cooed to the policeman. "I am sorry. I've come to see the owner of this newspaper, Mr. Terry Bigge. He's a friend of mine. Could you tell me where he is?"

The policeman looked her up and down. "Mr. Bigge's on his way to jail," he said stolidly. "He's under arrest." He took out a little black book. "Perhaps you'd like to leave your name?" he suggested.

Sheila Star's smile disappeared. Her jaw dropped. "Oh!" she squeaked, and backed away. "Oh, no, that won't be necessary!" She spun around and almost ran out the door, stumbling slightly as she went.

Tom made a rude noise. Miss Moss laughed maliciously. And even Zim managed a smile.

Sheila Star wouldn't feel like coming back to the *Pen* for a long, long time.

○

By the time the printers' trucks arrived and unloaded the new *Pens* half an hour later, things seemed more normal. A policeman was still on guard outside, but Zim was sitting at his desk and drinking a cup of coffee.

After the trucks had gone, we pulled down the roller shutter and held up the paper to show him. **GOLDEN PINES WILL SEN-SATION!** proclaimed the headline in thick black type. And underneath: **HEIRESS LEAVES GLEN TO PEOPLE.**

"Looks great, Dad," enthused Elmo.

Miss Moss, hovering around the back of Zim's chair, nodded vigorously. "It certainly does," she said. "It's a great issue."

Zim smiled ruefully, and stroked his tender throat. "Well, I'm glad," he said. "Since it'll probably be our last."

We fell silent, and he looked down into his cup, swirling the liquid around and around. "Got to face facts," he said. "Terry Bigge was right about one thing, at least. The printers can't go on carrying us. We're finished."

"You're forgetting about people paying for the paper this issue, Dad," Elmo objected.

Zim squeezed his arm. "Look, Elmo, and all of you," he said. "You know how much I appreciate all you've done. But I don't know that there's as much good feeling toward the *Pen* as you think. Especially lately. Dad was a great editor. But I . . ." His voice trailed off. He pressed his lips together.

"Anyway," he went on more briskly, "It's past nine. We're very late getting the paper out. So —"

The door in the roller shutter creaked open. Noise from the street beat in on us. "Excuse me, sir," called the policeman. "Ah — could you come here a moment?"

Zim heaved himself to his feet and walked over to him. We followed.

"What's gone wrong *now?*" muttered Nick.

21

Help for hire!

The policeman was jerking his head out through the door and into the street. "The lieutenant around the corner at the front entrance has been having a bit of trouble," he muttered, rubbing at his mouth to hide a smile. "Seems a few people want to buy a paper. He sent them around here. They say the delivery's late and they can't wait, so they've come here to buy in person."

Zim's eyebrows shot up in surprise. "Really?" he exclaimed. He popped his head out the door. There was a roaring noise. The policeman's grin broadened. Zim jerked back and spun around to us. His eyes were wide. His mouth was open. He couldn't speak. Just pointed.

So then we looked, too, and saw what he had seen. A chattering line of people that stretched up the street and around the corner. A cheering, chanting crowd waving money in the air. "Save the *Pen!*" they were calling. "Save the *Pen!*"

"Miss Moss!" squeaked Zim, clutching at his hair, and beginning to tear at the bundles of newspapers with his bare hands. "Get the petty cash box!"

But we didn't really need the petty cash box. No one wanted

change. They just wanted to donate some money to help. We worked frantically, but the more *Pens* we sold, the more people arrived to join the line, which soon snaked right around the corner and created chaos.

By lunchtime, the *Pens* were all gone. We put up notices to say so. We ran along the line, telling everyone. But then people started just coming in and handing over their donations without expecting anything in return. And almost every one of them had a word of praise for the paper, or a handshake for Zim, who simply stood, amazed, as the pile of cash grew.

When a nurse from Golden Pines came with a plastic bag full of coins from the residents, he was surprised. When Ralph Muldoon grandly jumped the line with Poopsie under his arm to hand over a hundred dollars, mumbling that "mistakes will happen" and "sorry to hear about the problems, my boy," he was astounded. When the manager of Molevale Markets came in with a check, he was flabbergasted.

"When you kids spread the word, you certainly spread the word," he muttered to us.

Nick puffed out his chest. "We're not called Help-for-Hire for nothing," he said.

○

So that's how the *Raven Hill Pen*, and the Glen, were saved. At the police station, Terry Bigge finally admitted everything and named the man who had helped him burn the office.

He tried to pull Sheila Star down with him, too, but no one really believed she'd had anything to do with the will or the fire.

She was just a mischief-maker who thought she was using Terry to get something she wanted. But all the time he was really using her, of course, to help him destroy the *Pen* and make sure old Mr. Zimmer's evidence against him was never found. She got off with a warning. Terry Bigge was sent to jail.

Zim made enough money that famous Thursday to give the printers everything he owed them. The insurance people paid up, and the *Pen* office was fixed and redecorated so that it was much, much nicer and brighter than it had been before. Miss Moss was nicer and brighter, too. She kept her plastic palm tree, though. She said it had even more sentimental value for her now.

I went on going to see Miss Plummer every week. But I never talked to her, or anyone, about the night I found her in the Glen.

I never talked to her about how odd it was that when the Golden Pines staff looked for her there, they couldn't see her. Almost as though someone was hiding her from them. I never talked about the soft wind that had stirred the leaves where there had been utter stillness a moment before. Or the chill breath that made me shiver. And I never mentioned the traces of sweet flower perfume that had filled the clearing. I thought I'd better not. Miss Plummer didn't wear strong perfume. But Ruby always did. She loved the scent of violets.

What I figured was, Ruby Golden had done what she wanted to do, and now she could be at peace. There was no need to start the whole thing up again. Besides, I had about as much on my plate as I could handle. We'd all had our pictures in the paper, you see. And so Help-for-Hire Inc. was launched in a blaze of publicity that opened even Richelle's eyes. For a minute.

I think the thing we were most proud of was our teamwork.

Because when you came to think about it, the different talents of all of us had played a part in solving the *Pen* mystery. And strangely enough it was the talents we *didn't* mention in our ad that were most important.

Tom's drawing of Sheila Star helped unmask Tonia, the spy. Sunny's gymnastics saved her and me from the fire. Nick's cool curiosity got us into Terry Bigge's office. My bleeding heart, as Nick insultingly put it, made me make friends with Miss Plummer, and go to look for her when she was missing.

And Richelle? Even her eye for clothes came in. Because I don't think she'd have even mentioned seeing Tonia at the Black Cat Café, if Tom's sketch hadn't gotten Sheila Star's blouse a bit wrong.

We asked Elmo to join us. He adds determination to the mix. I've never met such a determined boy. So there are six Help-for-Hire kids now. Just as well, too. We've been inundated with work since the story in the paper.

And it's not all babysitting and dog walking, either. Some of the things we've been asked to do would curl your hair! Even Nick says it's interesting. Mind you, as he says, it's hard to see how *anything* could outdo our first job.

But, as my mom says, you never know.

Help-for-Hire cracked their first case! Will they survive their next? Turn the page to find out what happens when Tom faces off with a strange new boss named Sid, a noisy puppet named Jacko, and a dangerous criminal known only as the Gripper....

EMILY RODDA'S
RAVEN HILL MYSTERIES

#2: THE SORCERER'S APPRENTICE

Emily Rodda and John St. Claire

SCHOLASTIC INC.

New York   Toronto   London   Auckland   Sydney
Mexico City   New Delhi   Hong Kong   Buenos Aires

Contents

1

The Gripper

The name Jack the Gripper started as a joke, but there was nothing funny about what the thief himself was up to. He was vicious, always attacking from behind, whipping his arm around his victims' necks, and pulling it so tight they couldn't breathe. There was also something poking the victim in the back — possibly the hard point of a gun barrel.

Then he'd grab their bag or wallet and whisper, "Now I'm going to let you live and you're going to shut up. Got it? Keep your eyes closed till you count to fifty!"

It was always the same method and the same words. By the time a victim finished counting, the Gripper was gone. And the strange thing was, nobody ever saw a man running from the scene of the crime. Nobody ever saw anything suspicious at all. It was like the Gripper disappeared into thin air.

He usually went for his victims after dark, but occasionally an old man or woman alone in a parking lot in broad daylight would be too much of a temptation for him. So he'd rip them off as quick as a flash — and still get clean away.

I heard this lady on a call-in radio show saying that she thought he had supernatural powers. That's what she thought, anyway. Of course, I don't believe in things like that. But even with cops crawling all over Raven Hill, the attacks continued and nobody ever saw a thing. The Gripper was smart, no doubt about that.

At first, there were robberies once or twice a week, but soon they were happening almost every day. The Gripper hadn't killed anyone yet, but the police were obviously worried that he might. The attacks were getting more violent. More and more victims ended up on the ground, gasping for breath, and had to be taken to the hospital for observation.

Of course, there were a lot of sick jokes going around at Raven Hill High. But we weren't kidding ourselves. Everybody was walking around town looking over their shoulders for Jack the Gripper — even us kids.

Anyway, let me tell you how Help-for-Hire Inc. got involved in all this. . . .

❂

It was Friday afternoon and I was sitting in English class about to die of boredom. Mr. Larson was going on and on in this really quiet voice like he was trying to hypnotize us or something. He's a nice guy, Mr. Larson, but his classes aren't what you'd call exciting.

You are getting sleepy, very sleepy, Tom, I was thinking.

No matter how hard I concentrated, my mind kept wandering. He might just as well have been talking to us in Mongolian.

When was that final bell going to ring?!

Richelle was sitting in front of me and a little to the side, studying her fingernails. Good old glamorous Richelle. She wasn't listening to a word of what Larson was saying, either, but she had this look on her face like she was really interested. She kept nodding her head as if she were agreeing with him.

Anyway, I opened my sketchbook and started drawing her. She looked kind of like Snow White or something. Her hair was all in one neat piece, like it was plastic or it was held together with a pint of hair spray. She must have spent three hours working on it before school to get it like that.

Richelle *always* looked great. She was one of those people who could get lost in a rain forest for a week and come out looking like a cover girl. And I'm the kind of guy who'd look grungy wearing a tuxedo. Not that I've ever worn a tuxedo.

She turned her head, saw what I was doing and gave me the dirtiest look. Sort of a how-dare-you-draw-a-picture-of-me-without-my-permission look. "Stop that!" she mouthed silently at me.

When was that bell going to ring? Maybe the clock was stopped.

Of the six of us in Help-for-Hire — me, Elmo, Liz, Sunny, Nick, and Richelle — Richelle is the one with the charmed life. Teachers eat out of her hand. She can do anything and not get busted.

Richelle: "I couldn't finish my homework because I broke a fingernail when I went to the airport to see my grandmother off to Paris."

Teacher: "That's OK, Richelle. Just hand it in when you can."

All right, that's a bit of an exaggeration — but only a bit.

121

I'm just the opposite. I'm always in deep trouble.

Me: "I'm sorry I didn't finish my homework, but my whole family was wiped out when a crop-dusting plane hit our house. What with four funerals in one day, there wasn't enough time to finish my assignment, but I'll hand it in tomorrow."

Teacher: "Too bad, Tom, but you should have allowed time for emergencies. I'm going to have to give you an F."

You just get a feeling that if a hundred-dollar bill fell from the sky it would land in Richelle's pocket. Or some guy would pick it up off the ground and say, "Excuse me, miss, but I think you dropped something."

Me, I'd probably get arrested for theft.

Cop: "I don't know who you stole it from, son, but you must have stolen it from somebody. Come with us to the police station. With any luck, you'll be out of prison in forty years with good behavior."

Anyway, there I was sketching Richelle and trying to listen to Mr. Larson when the kid behind me dropped a note over my shoulder and into my lap.

Carefully, I unfolded the paper and read it. It read:

New gig. Meet corner of Wattle & Burke
streets <u>right</u> after school. Don't go to the Glen.
Don't go home. Be there or beware!

The note was from Nick. It wasn't signed, but it was his handwriting. And who else would call a *job* a *gig*? I turned around and there he was at the back of the class ignoring me and pretending to listen to old Mr. Larson. Typical Nick.

Another Help-for-Hire job, I thought. *Good. I sure could use the money.* I gave Nick the thumbs-up and he just rolled his eyes like I shouldn't even be looking at him. He was as bad as Richelle.

"Tom Moysten!" Mr. Larson yelled. "You're not paying attention!"

I whipped around in my chair and closed my sketchbook.

"Yes, I am," I said.

(Laughter.)

"Then tell me what I just said."

You know how sometimes you can repeat what someone just said even if you didn't really hear it at the time? Well, I couldn't. Not this time, anyway.

"You said I wasn't paying attention," I said.

(More laughter.)

Mr. Larson wasn't amused.

"Oh, a comedian," he said. "Perhaps you'd like to stand up here and tell a few jokes."

"No, thanks."

"Afraid to make a fool of yourself?" he asked.

"No, that's your job," I said.

(Long, loud laughter.)

I really didn't mean to say it. It kind of just slipped out. Mr. Larson folded his arms and stared at me. I could feel myself blushing, which made everything worse.

Just then the bell rang. Everybody started packing up.

"Tom," Mr. Larson ordered. "Stay right where you are."

But I wasn't in deep trouble this time, not really. Mr. Larson just said he was going to let me off, but that I had to pay attention from now on.

"Yes, sir."

Mr. Larson isn't a bad person. He and Brian — that's my stepfather — are good buddies. Brian teaches ancient history at Raven Hill High. You always see him and Mr. Larson together in the staff room.

"And, Tom?"

"Yes?"

"You've got a good sense of humor."

"Thanks."

"But try not to use it all the time," he said. "Give it a rest."

"Yes, sir."

2

Help-for-Hire together

I ran to catch up with Nick and Richelle. They were chatting, heads together. Two of a kind.

When I got close, I realized that they were talking so much that they didn't see I was behind them. I couldn't help myself: I got really close and then put an arm around Richelle's neck.

"Close your eyes and count to fifty!" I whispered.

Of course, I didn't do it really hard and Richelle just turned around and gave me a shove.

"Cut it out!" she yelled. "That's not funny!"

"Grow up, Moysten!" said Nick. "And what are you doing here, anyhow? What's the story? Didn't Larson keep you in?"

"Only because he wanted my advice."

"Be serious!"

"Would I lie to you? He wants to know how to make his classes more entertaining," I said. "He asked me to help him develop his sense of humor. We start next week. It could take a while."

"You know what, Tom?" Richelle said. She was still rubbing her throat like I'd really hurt her — which I definitely hadn't. "You're a real jerk."

"I do my best," I said.

"And give me that!"

Richelle grabbed at the sketchbook but I put it behind my back. I knew she wouldn't try to fight me for it. That wasn't her style. Besides, it might mess up her hair.

"I just want to see the drawing you did of me," she said.

"It's not finished," I said.

"So what?"

"So you won't like it."

Nick glanced over like he was bored or something.

"Just show it to her, Moysten," he said.

"No way," I said.

Liz, Sunny, and Elmo were waiting at the corner up ahead. Here we all were: the whole Help-for-Hire gang together in the same spot at the same time. Considering it was Friday afternoon, this was pretty amazing. We were with them in a minute.

Liz was the first to speak.

"Thanks for coming," she said. "Sorry I couldn't give you any more warning. I got a phone call last night from Sidney Foy, the guy who owns Sid's Magic Shop across the street there."

I looked across at the row of old shops, most of them boarded up. The paint on Sid's sign was peeling so badly that you couldn't read all the letters. If you looked at it quickly, you'd think it read: ID'S MAG   HOP.

"Oh, that place," Nick said.

"He wants some help cleaning," Liz explained. "That's all he said. I don't know how much or what kind."

"Cleaning?" Nick said. "Well, that counts me out."

"What do you mean?"

"What do you mean, 'What do I mean?' Look at me. Do I look like a cleaning lady?"

"Hey! That's sexist!" Sunny objected.

"All right, a cleaning *person*, OK?"

"Well, if that's the way you feel, Nick, you shouldn't be in Help-for-Hire," Liz snapped. "Everybody does everything, OK? That's the deal. No picking and choosing. Otherwise, it's unfair. And bad for business, too."

Of course, Liz was right. I didn't mind the Help-for-Hire work, but Nick and Richelle only wanted to work when it was easy or fun. They probably got more allowance than the rest of us put together. Of course, they spent it as fast as they got it. Richelle had more new clothes than she knew what to do with. So did Nick, for that matter.

"I'm just no good at cleaning," Nick pleaded.

"Yeah, sure," said Sunny. "Like we are, right? Like we were all born with cleaners' chromosomes and you weren't, right?"

I liked the way Sunny didn't let him get away with anything.

"Are you in or out, Nick?" Liz asked. "Remember, if you're out, you're out for good."

Nick waited for a minute before answering and then said, "Oh, OK, I'm in. But I'm allergic to dust."

Everyone laughed.

"Come off it, Nick," Sunny said. "You're allergic to work, that's what you're allergic to."

"Sunny, that's not nice," Nick said.

I *am* allergic to dust — and grass and cats and dogs and you name it. But I didn't say anything. Partly because I didn't want

127

to sound like I was making excuses, but mainly because I *loved* the idea of working in Sid's Magic Shop. It was such a great place. I only lived a few blocks away, and I'd been in it lots of times though I can't say I spent a lot of money. It was just a good place to go to look around at everything.

"Right," Liz said. "Now let's go over and talk to Mr. Foy. We listen and then we talk about it between ourselves afterward, OK?"

"OK, Boss," Nick said meekly.

She gave him a crushing look and stalked off across the road.

○

There was definitely something strange about Sid Foy, or Sigmund the Sorcerer, as he was also known. That had been his stage name when he had a magic show that toured all over the country. He reckoned that he'd performed in every town and city with a population of more than two thousand. I didn't think that was possible, but I never knew what to believe when Sid was talking.

Anyway, he did all those old tricks like sawing someone in half and pulling pigeons out of his sleeves. And he was also a terrific ventriloquist. He had a dummy, Jacko, that he sat up on the counter, and sometimes when you asked Sid a question, the dummy answered.

So why did he stop doing his magic show and open a magic shop? Simple. He was in a car accident. He hit a deer late at night and the car went into a ditch and flipped over. He almost died from the injuries. When he got out of the hospital six months later, he was missing his right arm and his right eye.

He had an artificial arm with a sort of hook on the end instead of a hand, but he didn't always wear it. He also had an artificial eye, made of glass. It looked quite real, but I don't think he was comfortable with it, because a lot of the time he just wore a patch over his blind eye instead.

Now if all that happened to me, I reckon I'd just sit around and watch TV for the rest of my life and feel sorry for myself. Not Sid. Every time I'd been in the shop, he was laughing and joking like everything was OK. Well, maybe it was.

Anyway, that was Sigmund the Sorcerer.

3

The magic gig

You know how when you go into some shops there's a *ping* or a bell or a buzzer or something to say that a customer just came in? Well, Sid had one of those except it wasn't a *ping* or a bell or a buzzer — it was a shriek like in a horror movie followed by a mad, evil laugh. It was really great. Richelle went in first, and she wasn't ready for it. She jumped right back out the door, screaming.

Admittedly, Sid had the sound turned up too high and it really did give you a shock even if you knew about it.

"It's just a doorbell," I said, rubbing my foot where she'd trampled on it. "It won't bite you."

She shook back her hair and made a face. "How *stupid*," she said.

We all trooped in and looked around the dark and dusty room. A single light, dangling from a frayed cord, lit the middle of the shop. There was a counter over on one side.

"This place needs more than cleaning," Nick said. "It needs knocking down and rebuilding."

"Shhh!" ordered Liz.

There was no one else in the shop: no customers, no sign of

Sid. The place looked like something out of a science-fiction movie, all those horrible rubber masks on the wall and then shelves and shelves of things in boxes, collecting dust.

I started looking around at all the jokes and tricks: itching powder, rubber fingers, plastic ice cubes with spiders in them, drinking glasses with holes in them so everything dribbles down your shirt.

I picked up a huge rubber spider and held it out to Richelle.

"Tom! If you do, I'll kill you!" she screamed. "You put that thing down. Put it down!"

"I'm just showing it to you."

"Yeah, sure," she said.

"Mr. Foy! We're here!" Liz called out. "Help-for-Hire!"

No answer.

"He's probably gone out of business and turned into a hermit," Nick muttered. "Nobody ever comes in here. It's got to be the stupidest business in town. Kids don't want this old stuff. It's like something out of the Dark Ages. This isn't a shop, it's a museum."

"Nick!" Liz whispered. "He might hear you."

"So what if he does?"

"I like this place," I admitted.

"Do you ever come in here?" Nick asked.

"Sure."

"What's the last thing you bought in here?" he asked.

"I can't remember."

Nick gave me one of his smug looks. He was right, I hardly bought anything. But there was something about the place I liked.

"See? Museum," Nick said. "Everybody comes to look, but

nobody buys. Either this guy is rich and doesn't care how he makes a living or he's living on fresh air."

The others were looking around the shelves. Sunny picked up three rubber balls and started juggling them.

Richelle picked up a plastic cow. It mooed and stuck out its tongue.

"Oh, yuck!" she said. "That's plain *wrong!*"

"Let me tell you something, Tom," Nick said. "Any business that has to depend on kids' allowances is a stupid business. How much money can you squeeze out of a kid? They're always poor. It's parents who have dough. If I had a shop, I'd sell something that rich people buy, like Armani suits, Cartier watches, Gucci shoes, stuff like that — pricey things."

"Who's got money for those things in Raven Hill?" I asked.

"There are a few people," Nick said. "Anyway, who said anything about Raven Hill? I'd open a shop where the big money is. Look at this place, it's a hole. Kids come in here and play around with things, but they don't have any money. They probably break more than they buy."

Having gotten rid of the rude cow, Richelle was on the far side of the shop looking at the things on the counter. Propped up against the cash register was Jacko, Sid's ventriloquist doll. He had red freckles, a loony wise-guy sort of expression, and brown hair that stuck out all over the place.

"Look!" she laughed. "It's a Tom doll!"

"Very funny," I said.

As Richelle reached up to touch Jacko's face, his eyes snapped open.

"She touched me! She touched me!" Jacko yelled, his head swiveling from side to side. "I'll sue! Call the police!"

Richelle let out a bloodcurdling scream and fell back against a small table, knocking plastic snakes and cockroaches all over the place.

"That does it!" she yelled. "I'm getting out of here!"

"What a good idea," the dummy said. "Mind if I come, too?"

With that, Sid raised his head above the counter. He had on his black eye-patch and his shirtsleeve pinned to his shoulder.

Liz stared at him in disbelief.

"So this is Help-for-Hire Inc.," he said. "My, my, only six of you? I reckon this job could take the whole army."

"And the navy," Jacko said.

"Thank you, Jacko," said Sid. "But, seriously, there's only enough room back there for one or two people. Which one of you is Elizabeth Free?"

"I am," said Liz. "What sort of cleaning do you want us to do?"

"Didn't I explain that on the phone? No, I guess I didn't. Very forgetful, I'm afraid. Better follow me," he said, walking toward a door at the back of the shop with his hand still in Jacko's back. "There's a storeroom here at the back that needs a good clean out. I'm afraid it's full of . . . well . . . what can I call it?"

"Junk," Jacko said.

"Thank you, Jacko."

"You're welcome, Sid."

"But it's not *all* junk. There are some valuable treasures in there, so I don't just want to throw everything into the alley. So

I guess you'd call this a sorting and sifting job. I'll be here to give advice, but I can't lend a hand."

"You've only got one hand, Sid," Jacko said.

"You don't say, Jacko."

"I do say, Sid."

"But I can keep an eye on things."

"You've only got one of those, too, Sid," the dummy said.

"That'll be enough of that, Jacko," Sid said.

Richelle just rolled her eyes at the corny humor.

"This place has got to be a bit of a firetrap," Sid said. "When I lived in the apartment upstairs, I didn't care. So if the place went up, the place went up. It was just me and Jacko here and we're disposable."

"Speak for yourself, Sid," Jacko said.

"But now I've moved out to the trailer park and rented the apartment to a nice young couple. We can't have anything happening to them."

The storeroom was stacked from floor to ceiling with piles of boxes and magazines and old clothes. There was just a narrow aisle down the middle leading to the back door.

"You can see the problem," Sid said. "It's so cramped in here that I think only one or two of you can fit. I think there's at least a week's work for one person if he or she spends, say, two hours on it after school."

"At least," Nick muttered, looking around.

"So what'll it be?" Sid asked. "One person or two? And when can you start?"

Through the dusty window at the back I could see Sid's tenants go up the outside stairs to the apartment above. They looked like they were in their early twenties. He had his arm around her, helping her. She was obviously expecting a baby — *very* obviously.

Liz went into the storeroom, studying it for a minute. A mouse ran along the aisle and then disappeared. Richelle, standing beside me now, shuddered.

"Oh, yuck," she muttered.

"We'll have to discuss it, Mr. Foy," Liz said, coming back.

"Just don't leave me up in the air too long," said Sid. "I want to get this fixed up as soon as possible."

"Don't worry," Liz reassured him. "We won't leave you up in the air. I'll get back to you tonight."

"Up in the air?" Jacko exploded. "Get back to us? That's not a girl — that's a boomerang."

"Now, be polite, Jacko," Sid said.

"Sorry, Sid," said Jacko.

Later, out on the sidewalk, Nick turned to me. "Well? Did you figure out how he does it?"

"Does what?" I asked.

"Stays in business. It's the upstairs apartment. He moved out to the trailer park because it's cheap. He rents the apartment for more than he's paying and that's how he keeps the shop open."

"You're just guessing," I said.

"I'll bet I'm right," Nick answered.

4

A meeting at the *Pen*

Usually we hold our meetings in a place called the Glen, a patch of forest beside Raven Hill park. But this day Elmo had to get back to help his father at the *Pen* office. The *Pen* was his dad's newspaper. Since one of Help-for-Hire's jobs was to deliver it around Raven Hill every Thursday before school, Mr. Zimmer (we called him Zim) didn't mind us meeting there. In fact, Help-for-Hire Inc. had recently kept the *Pen* from going out of business, so everyone in the office was always nice to us.

"Come on, let's work this out quickly," Liz said when we were all together. "I've got to get out of here soon to do Miss Plummer's shopping."

"And I'm just really tired out," Richelle said. "If I don't get home and have a nap soon, I think I'll die."

Sunny had ducked into the bathroom and changed into her running gear so she could run home. There's a girl who loves to sweat! She's a fitness maniac. If she's not running, she's at a gymnastics class. If she's not at gymnastics, she's at a tae kwon do class learning how to kick people in the teeth (just in self-defense, she says). She only comes up to my shoulder, but she's a dangerous person to know. I wouldn't want her to lose her temper with me.

"Well, what do you think?" Liz asked. "An hour or two after school every afternoon for one or two people. Who wants it?"

"Not me," Richelle said. "That guy is weird! And that shop is really *wrong*!"

"How about you, Nick?"

"Not my style," Nick said coolly.

"Elmo?"

"I'll do it if you want me to, but I've got to help Dad on the paper Tuesday and Wednesday."

"Sunny?"

"I don't like that shop, either. I don't mind Mr. Sid, or whatever his name is —"

"Foy."

"— but the place gives me the shivers. It's so dark and stuffy and closed in."

"And did you *see* the people who live upstairs?" Richelle rolled her eyes.

"Yeah, what's wrong with them?" asked Liz.

"Talk about slobs. Especially her. That smock thing she was wearing — yuck!"

"Richelle, she's pregnant, for heaven's sake!"

"That's no excuse for looking like a slob. There are some really good maternity clothes around now."

"I don't know, Richelle. Sometimes I wonder about you," Liz sighed. "But we're not here to talk about that, anyway. We're here to see who wants some work. How about you, Tom?"

I didn't want to seem anxious, but I really wanted to work in the magic shop. Maybe Sid would give me a discount on some of the tricks and stuff.

"I wouldn't mind," I said casually. "Dust kind of bothers me sometimes, but that's OK. I think it could be kind of . . . enlightening."

A couple of the others laughed and, sure enough, I blushed. Why did I have to say "enlightening" when I just meant it would be fun?

"Tom, you're a real dork, you know that?" Nick said. "That place is about as enlightening as a funeral parlor."

"I'll do it," I said.

"What days?" Liz asked.

"I don't know. Every weekday, I guess."

"You can't," Liz said. "The agreement is that we only work three days' maximum. I'll do two days and you can do three. We each work two hours."

"Suits me."

"If there's anything that needs two people at a time, we can double up," Liz said. "It doesn't look like it's going to take that long. We should finish it in a week, like Mr. Foy said. You want to start on Monday?"

"Sure," I said, looking bored. "May as well."

The fact is, I could hardly wait.

✿

It was getting dark and I was still hanging around the office, giving Elmo a hand trying to get a program to run on the computer, when Zim came out of his office.

"Be careful on your way home, Tom," he told me. "The Gripper hit someone again last night, you know. A woman."

"Where?" I asked.

"Over near Memorial Park."

My house backed Memorial Park.

"We were just down that way," Elmo said, "at Sid's Magic Shop."

"The police said the victim had been to the ATM at Nationwide Bank. She's from the country — just down here for a week, poor woman. Hadn't heard about the Gripper. Apparently, he followed her till he knew it was safe to make his move."

"Is she OK?" Elmo asked.

"Bruised neck, but she didn't want to go to the hospital," Zim said. "We'll be finishing up in a couple of hours, Tom. Happy to give you a lift then if you want. You can call your mom and tell her you'll be late. I don't like the idea of you walking home on your own in the dark. Not with things as they are."

"I'll be OK," I said.

"Yeah, the Gripper only robs people who have money," Elmo laughed.

Or people he thought were carrying money.

I was not about to hang around for two hours even if I was a bit nervous about walking through Raven Hill in the dark. It was Friday night. I was hungry. I wanted to get home.

"I'll be OK," I said.

It was somewhere near the post office that I sensed that something was very wrong. . . .

5

The chase

A few cars passed by and then the streets were quiet. Most people were home now getting ready for their evening meals, watching the news on TV, just relaxing after work.

I rounded the corner at the Nationwide Bank, and the light from the ATM booth was shining out into the street. There was no one around. Since the Gripper went into business, no one in Raven Hill was game to take out money after dark unless they were with someone to stand watch.

About a block farther on, the streetlights were out. Only lights from the houses kept the street from total darkness.

Home was near, only about a five-minute walk if I took the shortcut through Memorial Park or fifteen minutes if I kept to the street and took the long way around. I'd make the decision on which way to go when the time came.

I didn't have to decide yet.

In a house I heard a woman yelling at her kids, telling them to turn down the TV. "That thing's loud enough to wake the dead!" she screamed. Her voice alone was loud enough to wake the dead.

As I crossed the street, I heard the slight scuffing sound of a shoe on the sidewalk behind me. I turned slowly, pretending to look in the windows of a house but really looking back out of the corner of my eye.

There was nothing there.

I started humming a tune and tried to remember where I'd heard it. It was one of those songs that gets stuck in your head and you automatically start singing or humming it every few minutes when you try not to. Song pollution.

The scuffing came again. This time I turned quickly to see if there was someone behind me.

There was.

A shape crossed the sidewalk and disappeared up a driveway beside a darkened house. Someone going home? It was a man, I was pretty sure of that from the way he moved. But how can you really tell?

Somehow, just seeing the figure made me feel better. I relaxed a little. It wasn't a ghost or a creature, it was a real person, someone taking in a trash can or checking the mailbox.

He wasn't coming after me. It wasn't the Gripper.

I turned onto Riley Street. I'd have to make a decision soon. The path through the park was only half a block away now. The streetlights were on and most of the houses had lights on in them.

Plenty of light.

If I was sure no one was following me, I'd duck down through the park and be home in no time at all. Memorial Park isn't very big. You'd be able to see the back of our house from the entrance if there weren't bushes and trees in the way.

If anything was suspicious, I'd just keep walking around the block and come in from the front. Ten more minutes, that's all. And there'd be houses all along the way and plenty of people to hear me if I yelled for help.

But I didn't want to give in to the fear.

I stopped and looked around. There was no one in sight.

No problems.

No one following me.

I stood there near the shortcut for a whole minute, looking around, peering in through the trees, listening for any sign of movement. Nothing. Not a thing. My stomach rumbled. If it had been some mad murderer running around Raven Hill killing people, then I wouldn't have gone in there.

But the Gripper wasn't a murderer — not yet, anyway.

He was a robber, a man who followed people who he thought had money in their pockets until he could get them alone. Usually women on their own.

I wasn't a woman.

I didn't have more than a couple of bucks on me.

He wouldn't want me.

I turned quickly and plunged down onto the dirt path and into the bushes. In a minute I was in the clearing where the play equipment was. Ahead I could see the dark silhouettes of the pine trees that guarded the little bridge across the gully. Home was a hop, step, and jump from the bridge. Everything was fine. I turned once or twice to make sure I wasn't being followed.

I began humming again and remembered where the tune came from. It was from a TV toilet paper commercial. How embarrassing. Don't want to get caught humming that at school.

I was laughing to myself when I heard the twig break.

I looked around quickly. Nothing moved. Maybe it was an animal. Maybe it wasn't.

The moon came out from behind a cloud and I could see the path better now. I started jogging and then heard the thud of footsteps somewhere behind me, somewhere in the distance.

Then I was running and the footsteps behind me were running, too, coming up fast. I turned quickly but looked back, afraid I'd hit a tree.

There was a man behind me and he was on the path, pelting toward me, gaining on me with every step.

I thought he was shouting at me as he ran, I heard a word — a couple of words — but I couldn't be sure with my blood pounding in my head, my lungs straining for air.

Who was he? Why was he chasing me? It couldn't be the Gripper. It couldn't!

This isn't happening, I thought.

I had my hands out in front of me, barely making out the path, hitting a bush and briefly bouncing backward.

Please, please let me outrun him.

Now I could see the glint of the moon shining on the handrails of the bridge. If I could only hurl myself between them I'd be across in four strides and then through the fence into my backyard. If I called for help now, someone might hear me. But if I yelled it might make him even angrier.

He might clobber me just to stop my screaming and he'd be gone, blending into the darkness of the trees, before help came.

My feet slapped the boards of the bridge. Nearly, nearly . . .

A figure loomed up in front of me, blocking my path.

6

Words, words, words

I yelled. A flashlight glared into my eyes.

"Police," barked the figure, and by then his partner was standing behind me.

I nearly collapsed with relief. "Oh," I said, gasping for breath. "I thought . . . you were him."

The police, of course, thought I was the Gripper.

They didn't get rough or anything, but I guess you couldn't blame them for being suspicious. I mean, they really didn't know what the guy looked like. I guess he couldn't have been young like me. But I'm tall, and in the dark they weren't about to take any chances.

They asked who I was and everything and they wrote it down. I didn't have any identification on me. I told them where I lived. OK, they said, and off we went. Weren't Mom and Brian surprised!

My half brothers — that's Mom and Brian's kids — thought it was really great, me coming home with the police and everything. Mom talked to the cops about me and asked what was happening about finding the Gripper, but she didn't use that name because she didn't want Adam and Jonathon to know what was happening. She said something like, "Do you have any clues about the guy?" She just called him "the guy."

"I'm afraid not," one of the cops said.

Adam's only five years old, but he made this incredible face. "Jack the Gripper!" he yelled. "Tom's Jack the Gripper!"

You had to laugh — and we all did, even Brian.

❁

Once the cops were out of the way, it was lecture time. Brian is big on lectures. I guess it's because he's a teacher or something.

"Ron Larson tells me you were entertaining his class today," he said.

"Yeah," I said.

I try to keep my answers short when Brian starts one of his lectures. It's useless trying to tell him your side of the story because he's always right. Arguing with Brian is like putting more wood on a fire. Just keeps him going.

"You know, you're a good kid, Tom," he said, "but you'll never get anywhere just being a good kid."

"I know," I said.

(Always best to agree with him.)

"You can't go through life being a comedian, Tom. Even comedians have to plan their lives. They have to take things seriously sometimes. They have to work hard at what they do."

"Yes," I said.

"The best ones study their craft intensely. You can bet your boots they take that studying seriously, too. They know it's going to be their bread and butter some day."

"Yes," I said.

"Don't you think it's time you started thinking about your bread and butter, Tom?"

"Yes."

Brian wasn't like my real dad. Dad would have at least given me a chance to explain. Not Brian. I mean, sure I got in trouble with Mr. Larson, but it wasn't any big deal. Everything was a big deal with Brian — especially when something happened at school.

"There were these two boys I taught in high school many years ago," he went on. "This wasn't in Raven Hill. They were both bright boys who could have really gone places. One of them listened in class and saved his jokes for when he was with his friends. The other one just couldn't help himself. He was always trying to be the class clown. He goofed off all the time. And you know what?"

Go ahead, tell me, I thought. *The one who goofed off got killed by a bank robber when he made a joke about the guy's ski mask, and the other one is the president.*

"Are you listening to me, Tom?"

"Yes," I said.

"The one who saved his humor for the appropriate moment went on to become a lawyer. Now he has a wife, three beautiful children, and a lovely home in a good suburb. He's set for life."

"How about the other one?" I asked.

"He started college, but he dropped out. Couldn't apply himself, I guess. Last I heard he was working on a ship, cleaning decks and polishing brass. He was sailing around South America somewhere. He's nobody, going nowhere. But he could have really been someone, Tom, if he had only kept himself under control."

Mom was fiddling with knives and forks on the table. She looked over at me and frowned. You could tell she didn't like Brian's lecture, either, but as usual she wasn't about to say anything. I sometimes wonder if she thinks she might lose another husband if she says what she thinks to Brian. Big loss.

"You mean," I said, "that if only the comedian had listened and not goofed off, he could be living in a posh suburb and going to the office every day in a suit. Right?"

"The day will come when you wish you could do that, too," said Brian. "Mark my words. There's still time, Tom, if you get your act together. You're a talented boy. You could make a valuable contribution to society."

Valuable contribution to society! That lawyer probably makes his money keeping gangsters from going to jail. Big contribution to society. But you can't talk about these things with Brian. I mean, what good does Brian do anyone? He teaches ancient history to a few kids and then comes home and sits in front of the TV and drinks beer.

"When they catch this Gripper guy," Brian said, "and look into his background, I'll bet your bottom dollar they'll find that he was once just an ordinary kid like you who couldn't apply himself."

An ordinary kid like me? I liked that.

"Now he's ripping off strangers because he's bitter about his failure, and it's the only way he knows of to get rich," Brian added.

Why was Brian always so depressing? What a difference from

147

Dad. Dad used to be an architect, but he stopped and became a painter. Now he lives over on the coast with Fay. She's an artist, too. Neither of them makes much money, but they like the way they live and that's all that matters to them.

I've heard Brian talking to Mom about Dad. Of course, he thinks Dad's a failure. I heard him say that Dad wasted a lot of taxpayers' money going to public school.

"What I'd like you to do, Tom," Brian said, "is to make yourself a promise right now. I want you to promise yourself that you'll take your studies more seriously, starting right now."

"OK."

"OK, what?"

"I will."

"Say it," Brian persisted. "Say, I promise — myself — that I won't be the class clown anymore."

"Why do you want me to say it out loud? I mean, it's a promise to myself, isn't it?"

"This way you won't forget. Say it."

This time he'd gone too far. I didn't want to get in a fight, but I wasn't about to let him do this to me, either.

Adam and Jonathon were arguing over the TV remote while all this was going on. They were good kids — considering they were *his* kids. Heaven help them when they got older and had to make promises to themselves for Brian's sake!

I started thinking about the sailing comedian. I hope he started his own comedy club in Rio, got rich and famous, and now he's the president of Brazil. That's what I'd like to think, anyway. Or maybe he's just lying on a beach somewhere telling jokes to the seagulls and having a good time.

"Well, Tom?" Brian asked.

Now I could feel my head heating up and I knew I wasn't blushing. I was getting really angry and I knew what I had to do — get away.

I stood up and headed for my room.

"It's time to think very seriously about your life, Tom," he called after me. "It really is."

Someday I was going to start thinking very seriously about a life a long way away from Brian and Raven Hill.

South America, here I come!

7

Help-for-Hire overload

We were having a very quiet dinner. Brian wasn't talking to me and Mom wasn't talking at all. Only Adam and Jonathon were talking and I guess they were making up for the rest of us.

The phone rang and I picked it up.

"Just got a phone call from a lady," Liz told me. "It's a child-care job. Babysitting, OK?"

"Why not?" I said.

"Just one kid but his mother wants two of us at a time, every weekday from three-thirty to five-thirty for two weeks. She's willing to pay double our usual fee."

"Double because there's two people or double double?"

Brian gave me this really hard have-her-call-back-after-dinner look and I ignored it.

Mom had her hands full helping Jonathon and trying to convince Adam that people who never eat vegetables stay five for the rest of their lives. Well, that's not exactly what she was telling him, but it might just as well have been.

"Double double," Liz said. "She wants two of us and she's willing to pay us *each* double."

"What's the catch?" I asked.

"None that I know of. Well, we're supposed to take him out, like walking around or something. We can take him to our own houses if we want. She doesn't want him cooped up in her place all the time, which is fair enough."

"Everybody's going to want this one," I said.

"Yeah, I know. It could cause problems."

"Where does she live?" I asked. Maybe that was the catch.

"Her name's Mrs. Anderson," said Liz. "She lives in that row of apartments behind Sid's Magic Shop. There's an empty lot and then there's the apartments. You know?"

"Anderson?" I asked. "What's the kid's name?"

"Timmy."

That was the catch.

"Hold on!" I said. "*Timmy Anderson?* Did you say Timmy Anderson?"

"Yes. He's a real little —"

"He's a real little something all right. No way, Liz. That kid's a monster."

"He can't be all that bad."

"He is, Liz! The kid's impossible. It would take four of us — one to hold each arm and leg — to control that kid. You look after him if you want to, but I don't want anything to do with him."

"His mother told me he was shy. She said he was very sensitive."

"Shy? Sensitive? The kid's only been in Raven Hill for six months and I think he's already got a criminal record."

"Tom, he's only seven! You make him sound like a gang of

Hell's Angels or something. She says that he's very creative and she wants to make sure he has a chance to express his creativity."

"Liz, he's in Jonathon's class. He steals everything that's not nailed down. He's a bully and a con man. He's creative all right, but not the way his mother thinks. Jonathon, come over here and tell Liz about Timmy Anderson."

Jonathon jumped down from the table and came to the phone.

"Hey! Where are you going, young man?" Brian called.

"It's important," I said. "It'll just take a sec."

God, I wish that man would just relax for a second. Did he think his kid was going to starve to death?

I handed the telephone to Jonathon.

"Hello . . . yes?" he said. "Timmy showed his bottom . . . No, his bottom . . . to cars . . . yes, lots of things . . . no. I don't know."

"Tell her about all the other stuff he does at school," I whispered. But it was no use. Jonathon was listening without saying anything. He's a real little talker usually, but give him a telephone and he clams up.

"I'll take it, Jonno," I said, grabbing the phone and sending him back to the table.

"I'll tell you later, Liz," I said in a low voice. "The point is, the kid's uncontrollable. This is a job we ought to turn down."

"It's only for two weeks," Liz said. "What could go wrong?"

"What," I asked, "after he burns down our houses? Well, I suppose he could always kill us."

"What's gotten into you?" Liz asked. "Where's the jokey, jolly Tom?"

"Sorry. I guess I'm just all joked out," I said. "But I really don't want the job myself."

"I can only do two days because of Miss Plummer, delivering the *Pen*, and cleaning the magic shop. But the others'll love the chance to make that much money," Liz said. "Let's meet at the Glen tomorrow morning at ten. We'll work it out then, OK?"

"Fine."

"You call Sunny and Elmo and I'll contact the others."

❁

Liz was right about me not being myself.

I knew it, and so did Mom. She had a talk with me later in my room and asked if I wanted to visit Dad during break. She didn't realize that the real reason I was on edge wasn't Brian or school or anything — it was the Gripper. After the chase with the cops, I just didn't seem to be able to get the guy out of my head.

Maybe I knew then what would finally happen. . . .

8

The plan

"What's this about bare bottoms?" Nick asked me. "Is this another one of your jokes?"

The others were all waiting there at the Glen when I arrived.

"That Timmy kid," I said. "My little brother said he was dropping his drawers to passing cars right in front of the school."

"So you reckon that if he doesn't murder us he'll embarrass us to death, is that right?"

"You do what you want," I said. "I'm staying out of this one."

"OK," said Liz, "who wants some of the babysitting and to earn a fortune?"

"Me!" said Nick.

"And me," said Richelle.

"And me," said Elmo.

"Sunny told me she wants to do some, too," Liz said, looking over at Sunny who was pulling a pen and some paper from her bag. "I don't mind helping if Tom doesn't mind doing the magic shop on his own."

"No, that's fine with me," I said. "I'll work the whole five days."

Of course, I liked the idea of working in the magic shop, but I also liked the idea of seeing less of Brian for a while.

"We're only supposed to work three days a week," Liz said doubtfully. "Still, just this once . . . Sure your mom won't mind?"

"Nope," I said. I crossed my fingers.

"Remember, you've got the *Pen* delivery before school on Thursday as well. This could cut into your study time. No big assignments due?"

"Nope."

"Tom doing homework!" Elmo said. "Not very likely!"

"That's enough," said Liz. "Everyone wants a piece of the babysitting except Tom. Two people at a time. Elmo's busy Tuesday and Wednesday. I'm busy Friday. Richelle's got dancing class. Sunny's got gymnastics and tae kwon do. We've got that dog walking every day — um . . ." She frowned in concentration. "So that means . . ."

"You and Elmo watch Timmy Anderson on Monday," interrupted Sunny, who'd been quietly working it out on a piece of paper. "And Richelle walks the dog. Richelle and Nick watch Timmy on Tuesday, and I walk the dog . . ."

Her calm voice went on. She had it all organized. She'd thought of everything. Liz sat back in relief. So did I. My five afternoons at the magic shop were safe.

"Is that OK with everyone?" Liz asked, after Sunny had finished. "You've all got three afternoons' work a week except Tom, who has five. I've got four. That's all right. This is an emergency.

Now look, no changes unless they're absolutely necessary, or we'll get into a mess. OK?"

"Aye, aye, Captain," Nick said, saluting.

○

Sunny had jogged to the Glen. It was cool so she was wearing her winter running gear. When everyone else left, I asked her if she minded if I did a sketch of her.

"Sure," she said, "but make it really quick because I have to visit my great-grandmother."

"I'm the quickest draw in this here town, pardner," I said, pulling out a pencil and opening my sketch pad. "Just sit on the grass facing me. I'm only going to do your face, OK?"

Sunny's a good friend. I always feel safe with her — even if her mother *is* our family doctor.

Her father's Roy Chan, a quite famous Australian tennis player. He and Sunny's mother split up years ago and he moved back to Australia to work as a coach. I guess the divorce thing makes Sunny and me feel like we have something in common that the others wouldn't understand.

Sunny's dad remarried, but her mom hasn't. Sometimes Sunny worries that she's lonely — as if that were possible with patients yakking at her all day and five daughters raving on all night!

"She should get married again, too," Sunny often says. "But she says there aren't any good men around."

"She can have Brian," I tell her.

"Thanks, but no thanks," she says.

Sunny's no fool.

○

"How's the drawing coming?" Sunny asked after a while. "I've really got to go."

"It's OK," I said, "but it would be easier if you grew a beard."

Why do I say these stupid things?

"Am I that ugly?" Sunny asked.

Of course, Sunny has a really nice face and I wanted to say so, but I just couldn't.

"No," I said. "It's just easier to draw faces that have lots of lines and moles and beards and all that."

I showed her the drawing and she seemed to like it so I gave it to her. Then I told her about the police chasing me last night. I didn't tell her how scared I was. I made it sound funny.

We started talking about the Gripper. She said she wasn't worried because she thought she could outrun him.

"Did you hear about the woman he tried to rob last night?" I asked.

"Another one?"

"Yeah. She was putting out her trash can. Like, the street was really dark because the streetlights were out. She was in her nightgown and she decided that nobody would see her so she just went out to the sidewalk in her nightgown."

"What!?"

"Yeah. In her nightie. The Gripper came up and grabbed her from behind, but she got away."

"How'd she do that?"

"She gave him the slip."

"How?"

"The slip. Get it? Her slip. She gave him the slip?"

"A slip is different from a nightie!" she said, and then she burst out laughing anyway.

I knew there was another reason Sunny was a good friend — she laughed at my jokes.

9

Magic, magic, magic

I usually hate Monday mornings. Come to think of it, I'm not big on Tuesday, Wednesday, Thursday, or Friday mornings, either. But this Monday morning, I woke up before my alarm went off and was up and dressed in a flash.

The day flew by, and after school I headed for the magic shop. Liz and Elmo walked along with me. They were on their way to pick up Timmy from school. They were going to take him back to Liz's place till Timmy's mother got home from work.

Elmo told us about the latest Gripper attack. This time it was an old man, a doctor, who was going to someone's house. The Gripper caught him just as he stepped out of the car. He took the doctor's wallet and his medical bag.

"I think he was after the drugs," Elmo said. "He's got to be a junkie. Why else would he need all that money?"

Elmo had a point.

Nobody mentioned Timmy. I have to admit I was secretly hoping he'd give them a lot of grief. Nothing too bad, mind you, but if he was a perfect angel, it was going to make me look pretty stupid after I'd badmouthed the kid.

✻

Sid was there behind the counter when I entered the shop. The laughter from the door nearly made me laugh, too.

Sid had his artificial arm on and it had those curved metal pincers on it — sort of like a hook, but it wasn't sharp and it opened and closed, if you know what I mean. He was holding a piece of paper and there were lots of little receipts lying in piles in front of him.

There was no one else in the shop.

"Tax time," he said.

He slipped his arm into Jacko's back.

"He just loves it when it's tax time," Jacko said. "It gives him something to do."

"That'll be enough, Jacko," Sid said.

"Tom, did you hear the one about the woman who bought a hat?" Jacko asked me. "The salesman said, 'That'll be twenty-five dollars plus tax.' And she said, 'Forget the tacks, I'll nail it to my head!' Ha-ha-ha-ha! Get it? 'Forget the tacks —'"

"Thank you, Jacko," Sid said, looking up. "But I don't think Tom came to hear your corny jokes, did you, Tom?" He took his arm out of Jacko's back. "In fact you probably couldn't even hear it because your ear was blocked."

With this, Sid reached over the counter and pulled an egg out of my ear.

"Now, that's better, isn't it?"

"Hey!" I said. "How did you do that?"

Sid had this long, rolling kind of laugh that sounded kind of phony, but it never failed to make me laugh, too. I guess it was something he used in his act to get the audience laughing.

"Nothing to it, my boy," he said. "Just a little example of Sigmund the Sorcerer's sleight of hand."

"He's slight of hand, all right," Jacko said. (This time Sid didn't bother to put his hand in Jacko or work his mouth.) "He's so slight of hand he only has one of them. Ha-ha-ha! That's what I call slight of hand!"

"Now, now, Jacko," Sid said. "No hand jokes, please."

"Sorry, Sid."

"That's more like it."

I had to admire Sid. There he was with one arm and one eye and a shop that couldn't have been making a cent. Probably Nick was right, and the only real income he had was the rent from the upstairs apartment.

He must have been a real optimist. Not like me. I like people who always look on the bright side of things — but I don't think I could ever be one. It's interesting, though. Lots of people think I'm always in a good mood because of the jokes and stuff.

Little do they know.

"Ever see the shell game?" Sid asked, putting three plastic cups on the counter. Then he took a furry red ball out of his pocket and put it next to one of the cups.

"I saw this on TV once," I said.

"Put the ball under one of the cups."

I did what he said.

"Now keep both eyes on the cup with the ball under it."

"Which is more than *you* can do, Sid," Jacko's voice said.

"That'll be enough, Jacko."

161

"Sorry, Sid."

Sid slid the cups around the counter one at a time, very slowly, and then lined them up again in a row. I didn't have any trouble keeping track of the cup I'd chosen. I made sure he didn't push the cup toward the edge of the counter to let the ball fall to the floor.

"You think it's under this one, don't you?" he said, getting ready to lift the one on the right end of the row.

"No," I said, pointing to the one in the middle. "It's under that one."

"That's funny," he said, lifting the end cup, "I was sure . . ."

Sure enough, the red ball was under the end cup. Then he lifted the cup on the other end and there was another red ball. Finally, he lifted the one in the middle and there was another red ball.

"Goodness!" he exclaimed. "Where are they all coming from? They must be breeding in the dark or something."

How did he do it? I have no idea. Sid just gave me a big smile and said in his Jacko voice, "It's magic! Do you believe in magic, Tom?"

For the moment I did. At least I wanted to.

"But you're probably itching to get to work on that storeroom," he said. "When you have some time, I'll teach you a few of the tricks of the magic trade."

"Do you mean it?" I asked.

"Of course I do," he answered. "Now about the storeroom . . ."

"What about it?"

"I have a confession to make. I don't even know what's in there. I'm about the world's most forgetful and disorganized person. And on top of that, I hate throwing stuff away — I save everything. So I'm going to leave it to you. Have a good look around in there and give me your advice, OK?"

10

Puzzle soup

I spent the next hour just looking through the junk in the storeroom. Well, it wasn't all junk.

There was everything in there: games that weren't selling, old books on how to do magic tricks, broken dress dummies from when the place had been a clothing store, an old fridge, pieces of a car engine. You name it, it was in there. Piles and piles of it.

"Your considered opinion, sir," Sid said. "The easiest thing would be to just kick it all to the curb, wouldn't it? Take it out in the alley and leave it for the garbagemen."

"I wouldn't," I said. "There's a lot of good stuff in there: things you could fix up and sell in the shop or just put ads in the *Pen* and sell. You could even have a yard sale."

"Spoken like a true collector. Your room at home isn't as messy as this by any chance?"

He wasn't wrong about that. At least I'm sure Mom would have agreed with him.

"I don't like to waste things if someone else can use them. And why throw away money?"

"What would you keep?"

"Well, there's a pile of old masks. I suppose I could clean them up and they'd still be good. You could sell them cheap. And jigsaw puzzles. There's a pile of them. I opened the boxes and they looked OK. It's just that someone cut the tape and opened them. We can tape them closed again, can't we?"

"Oh, them. I'm afraid they're not OK. You see, there's a little kid who used to come in here. He never bought anything. He just played around quietly down behind the shelves. Little did I know that he was up to something. Then one day a customer returned a jigsaw puzzle because there were pieces missing. Fair enough. There weren't just pieces missing, there were other pieces from other puzzles mixed in. That little so-and-so scrambled all the puzzles!"

"What a —"

"And that's not all. When he finished with that, he did the same with the games: the wrong dice in the wrong boxes, things like that. And *that*'s not all. He mixed up some of the powders in the makeup kits and then he cut the legs off some of those rubber spiders. That little troublemaker must have cost me a small fortune."

"Did you tell his parents?"

"Yes, and they offered to pay, but I didn't know how much to ask. Besides, I felt partly to blame because I'd let him get away with it. So I said, 'Just please don't let him come in the shop ever again.' And do you know what his mother said?"

"What?"

"She said he was a very creative child. 'Creative!' I said. 'If he's creative now I just hope he never gets to be destructive.'"

"Timmy Anderson," I sighed.

"How did you know?"

"He's got a certain reputation," I said.

○

I put the puzzles aside and looked through the magic sets. One of them had three magic wands and no rope for the rope tricks. Another box was filled with just bits of rope. All the instruction books were in a third box. I sorted things out and Sid got out his heat-sealer and sealed each set in plastic so it looked like it was new.

"I'll mark these down," Sid said. "That way if there's still anything wrong with them people won't feel they've been cheated. Got to keep the customers happy. Don't want to drive them away."

Then he said, in his Jacko voice, "I used to make a lot of money driving customers away."

"You did? How'd you do that?"

"I was a taxi driver! Ha-ha-ha-ha."

"That'll be enough of your corny jokes, Jacko," Sid said.

There was another thing I liked about Sid besides his cheeriness and his optimism. He had a shop to look after and a living to make and he had to do his taxes and all that, but all the same he just wasn't like the other adults I knew. You could talk to him the way you talk to one of your friends. It was like he was sort of half kid. Like you didn't have to pretend with him.

I got a bucket of soapy water and started cleaning a pile of old rubber masks: Dracula, the Frankenstein monster, and just plain horrible faces. Some were so old that they cracked and tore when I washed them and I had to throw them away.

Behind the masks I found a box of itching powder.

"You can have it, Tom," Sid said. "Nobody buys things like that anymore."

"Thanks," I said, slipping it into my pocket. "I'll find a use for it."

"Now, unless you want to spend the night with the mice, you'd better get yourself cleaned up and go home."

The two hours had gone by so fast that it seemed like only half an hour! When I came out of the storeroom, it didn't look much better than it had when I started. Sid was back to working on his taxes. He handed me an envelope with my two hours' pay.

"It isn't much," he said. "But you earned every cent of it."

"I'm afraid I didn't make much of a hole in the mess," I said. "I hope I can finish it all in one week."

"Don't you worry about that," he said. "Things take time. You want to get anything done in life, you've got to be prepared to work and be patient."

It was the same sort of thing that Brian might have said, but coming from Sid, somehow it sounded OK.

"See you tomorrow," he said.

And that's when I heard the screams.

11

The terror of Timmy

The screams were coming from behind the shop. I ran back through the storeroom and peered out the filthy window into the alley. There in the semidarkness were Liz and Elmo each pulling the screaming Timmy along by his arms. With their other hands, they were clutching bits of clothing.

Timmy was naked except for his underpants.

"I don't want to go home!" he screamed. "Don't take me home. I'll kill you! I'll kill you!"

I burst out laughing.

Sid looked up from his work as I passed the counter again. "Did I hear a familiar voice?" Sid called out.

"You did," I said. "Two of the gang — Liz and Elmo — are babysitting him."

"Oh, lucky them."

○

That night I carried all seven jigsaw puzzles home with me and took them to my room. Brian was too busy watching the news to notice and Mom was in the kitchen. Good thing.

Anyway, I cleared everything off the floor and dumped the puzzles into seven separate piles. Seven one-thousand-piece puzzles all mixed up together. Seven thousand pieces! This was going to be fun.

As I worked away on them, I kept laughing to myself about Timmy. I wanted to phone Liz and ask her about it but I wanted to see her face.

After a while there was a knock at the door. I don't know how you can tell from a knock, but I knew right away it was Jonathon.

"I'm busy," I said.

I could hear Mom calling out to him to leave me alone because I was studying.

"Can I come in?" Jonathon asked.

"I'm busy."

"I want to come in."

"What do you want?"

"I want to tell you a joke."

Most of the pieces in the pile I was working on were from a jigsaw puzzle of a zoo. I was busy picking out odd bits that belonged to one of the Milky Way.

"Tell me, then," I said. The least I could do was encourage his sense of humor. His father certainly wouldn't.

There was a silence and then Jonathon said, "The robber is joking people."

"What?"

I opened the door and pulled him into the bedroom.

"Don't say anything about the puzzles," I said. "Now what are you going on about?"

"You know the robber?" he asked.

I guess they must have been talking about Jack the Gripper even in Raven Hill Elementary School.

"Yes, I've heard about him."

"Well, he's killing people with jokes," Jonathon giggled, and looked at me expectantly.

It was a joke that was going around his school. Jonathon didn't understand it so he wasn't telling it right. I had to put it back together like a jigsaw puzzle. This was it: Did you hear that the Gripper has become a comedian? Now he's *joking* people to death. (Joking, choking — get it?)

"Good one, Jonathon," I said. "Keep working on it."

I filed it away in my brain to tell at school the next day.

○

I ran to catch up with Liz the next morning, just as she was going into Brian's history class. I tried to keep a straight face, but when she turned and I saw the scratches on her face it wasn't easy.

"Any trouble with Timmy?" I murmured.

She gave me this really dirty look like she didn't want to talk about it.

"I was just wondering," I said.

"Oh, shut up, Tom. It's not funny," she snapped.

"Touchy, touchy."

By lunchtime, everybody in the school knew what had happened. Timmy had been OK on the way to Liz's house. When he got there, he decided he wanted to make pancakes. When Elmo tried to talk him out of it, he completely lost it. He smashed every egg in the fridge, threw flour all over the carpets, and, while Elmo and Liz were cleaning up, he fed a whole cherry pie to Liz's dog.

When it was time to go home, Timmy refused to go. He said he wanted to live at Liz's house for the rest of his life. The only way Elmo and Liz could get him out the door was to tell him they were taking him to play on some swings. There was a little park near his apartment so they took him there.

When they got there, he started running around in circles saying that he wasn't going home ever again. Then he climbed up this really tall tree and started stripping and throwing his clothes all over the place. Liz and Elmo finally talked him into coming down, but Liz had to climb up and get the clothes that were stuck in the branches.

"She insisted," Elmo told Sunny. "I was for leaving the clothes up there and letting his mother go after them."

In English, I drew a cartoon of Timmy in his underpants and Liz and Elmo pulling him along the street. I gave him this huge mouth. Then I made up a poem and wrote it underneath. It went like this:

"A shy little fellow named Tim
Went off to have fun on a whim.
He climbed up a tree,
Then he yelled, 'Look at me!'
And he hung all his clothes from the limb."

Not bad except for the bit about "whim" and "limb." Well, I'm not Shakespeare, am I?

I held it out for Liz to see and she squinted over at it and then looked away again like she didn't even see it. She was really, really annoyed.

She turned back and said, "Sometimes you go too far, Tom!"

She was probably right and I felt kind of bad about rubbing it in. I tried to make everything OK at recess.

"So what did Mrs. Anderson say when you got back to her place?" I asked.

"She was just worried because it was after dark and because of all the robberies and stuff."

"Liz," I said, "I've got one piece of advice."

"What's that?"

"Drop him. He's too much trouble." No sooner were the words out of my mouth when I thought: *Ooops! What if they give up babysitting for Timmy and they all want to share my magic shop job?*

Luckily, Liz said, "Nick and Richelle have him this afternoon. Nick's not worried about it. He says they'll keep Timmy in line. He thinks Elmo and I were too soft on him."

"What's he going to do, glue the kid's clothes on?" I asked.

12

Tom the prestidigitator

That afternoon at the shop, Sid kept telling me to take breaks so he could show me how to do more magic tricks. And he was paying me by the hour. I guess Nick was right about Sid not being a very good businessman. But I was having a great time!

He showed me how to make things disappear. It was usually the same trick: You took a coin, for example, and while you were talking about what you were about to do you passed it from one hand to the other very casually. Of course, you didn't really put it in the other hand.

He was wearing his artificial arm, so he put the coin in the pincers at the end and then pretended to pass it to the other hand. It didn't work, of course, because you could still see where the coin was.

"It helps to have two hands," Jacko said.

I couldn't help laughing whenever Jacko said anything. He had a really quick, funny way of saying things. It was kind of sick, because I was laughing at Sid having only one hand, but, of course, it was Sid who was making the jokes.

It was really strange, eerie almost — like there were two people there in the shop, with different personalities. Maybe good ventriloquists really do develop double personalities after a while.

Anyway, Sid went on explaining the disappearing coin trick to me.

"The audience isn't expecting anything," Sid explained, "because they don't think the trick has started. They're still waiting for you to do whatever it is that you're going to do and, actually, you've already done it."

"Like, the coin's already in the wrong hand," I said.

"Exactly. From there you can quietly drop it in your pocket and get it out of the way. Then you just pretend to throw it up in the air with your empty hand and, of course, there's nothing there. Magic."

I tried the trick a couple of times, but it didn't look very convincing.

"Practice, my boy. Practice," Sid said. "I'll turn you into my apprentice in the art of prestidigitation yet."

"The art of what?"

"Prestidigitation. Presto, fast. Digits, fingers. Fast fingers. The art of fast fingers. Conjuring. Magic tricks have everything to do with making people believe what isn't true. Lying with your hands. But, of course, the fun of it is the window dressing, the way you make the tricks *look*. And the jokes. Humor has a lot to do with the fun. I know you're a man who likes to joke."

"Yeah, I do," I said. "I'm afraid I waste a lot of time telling jokes."

"Hogwash! Making people laugh is never a waste of time, Tom. Sigmund the Sorcerer loved a good joke and everybody loved Sigmund the Sorcerer."

Then he said in Jacko's voice: "What do you get when you drop a sorcerer on a land mine?"

"I give up," I said.

"A flying sorcerer. Ha-ha-ha! Get it? A flying sorcerer — a flying saucer. Sorcerer. Saucer. Ha-ha-ha."

"That'll be enough of that, Jacko," Sid said.

"It must have been great being a magician and traveling all around," I said.

"It was. I loved it. And I got to be pretty well known, especially in the country areas. Just between you and me, it wasn't the best-paying job in the world. Sometimes I'd get a big crowd and sometimes it was rainy and cold and nobody would come. It was a gamble, really. But life's not much fun if it isn't a gamble, I always say. You'll never get what you want if you don't take a chance."

✿

Bit by bit I was getting the storeroom cleaned out. There was a huge heap of garbage now in the alley out behind the old wooden fence. There were lots of things that couldn't be fixed — like two dozen legless spiders — but I convinced Sid to put some other things that were only a little bit damaged into a bin with a sign that said: EVERYTHING $1.

Once I'd cleared away a lot of the stuff, I found the equipment that Sigmund the Sorcerer had used in his act, like a box for sawing someone in half and a lot of juggling rings and balls. And there were some striking old posters of Sid. One of them had him in a black cape and top hat and in the other one he was wearing a white suit and a red turban.

"You can't throw this out," I said.

"Why not?" he said. "It's no good to me now."

"Can I have it?"

"What? That old stuff? Certainly not. Your mother would be down on me like a ton of bricks if I let you clutter up her house with my junk."

It probably would have been Brian and not Mom, but he was right, of course.

"You could keep them. There'll be plenty of room when I get this cleared away," I said hopefully.

"Remember the fire regulations, Tom," he said. "I say, chuck it all. We can't have this place going up in smoke just because some sentimental old fool wants to hang on to his past. Now get yourself tidied up and get out of here."

I felt really sad for old Sid. Now that I knew him better, I could see that he hid his real feelings a lot of the time. Just like I did. He acted like he didn't care, but underneath it all you could tell that he did. He cared a lot.

13

Good news,
bad news

That night Sunny called. She was dying to tell me what had happened to Nick and Richelle when they looked after Timmy.

"Which do you want first: the good news or the bad news?" she asked me.

"Give me the bad news," I said gleefully.

"No, I'll give you the good news: They managed to keep Timmy's clothes on. That's about the only good part."

"How about the bad news?"

Sunny giggled.

"He painted Nick's house."

"Painted his house? The whole house?"

"No, silly. Let me tell you. They picked him up from school and took him to Nick's place. Nick wanted to show Richelle some movies he'd made."

"I didn't know Nick had a camcorder."

"Oh, Nick's got everything," Sunny said. "OK, so they get to the house and Nick's mother isn't home. Nick warns Timmy not to get up to anything if he knows what's good for him. He says he isn't going to take any nonsense. He says he'll give Timmy a dollar if he's good."

Typical Nick, I thought. *Money's always the answer with him.*

Sunny went on. "So Nick starts showing Richelle the movies, and they don't realize anything's wrong till they turn around and see bubbles coming out of the aquarium — like, masses of soap bubbles foaming up and going all over the floor. Timmy's squirted dish detergent in the water."

"You're joking!"

"And then —"

"The house painting," I reminded her.

"Then," Sunny continued, "after Nick has rescued the fish that haven't died, he puts Timmy in a bedroom with some books and tells him to stay there or die. Then he and Richelle start cleaning out the fish tank. By the time they've finished, it's time to take Timmy home. So they go to get him."

I could hear Sunny take a breath and start to giggle again.

"There he is, still sitting on the bedroom floor where they'd left him. But then they see there's paint on his shirt. 'What's this?' Nick says. And after a while, they work out that the kid's climbed out the window and found a can of paint and some brushes in the garage. More mess, thinks Nick. But it isn't till they go outside that they see what Timmy's actually done. Right across the front of the house, in huge black letters, is: NICK STINKS."

I laughed. Quite a lot. I couldn't help myself. "Well, the kid's creative, all right," I said finally. "You've got to give him that. Did they manage to get the paint off?"

"Nick scrubbed it with turpentine. He got most of it off before his mother came home. I don't think Richelle did much."

So much for being tough with Timmy.

"So who has him tomorrow?" I asked.

"Guess."

"You?"

"And Liz. And he's *not* going home to my place."

"So what are you going to do with him? Mrs. Anderson wants him to get out and be creative."

"Liz and I think we just have to tell Mrs. Anderson that we stay at her place or we don't look after the brat. There's just no other way. And we may not be able to do the whole two hours."

"Why not?"

"Mom doesn't want me coming back after dark."

"Why not? It's only just getting dark when you finish."

"The Gripper, what else?"

"But as long as you're not alone and you're a kid —"

"Mom was talking to one of the police. Someone else was robbed last night. It was one of the lawyers in the Jubilee Building. He was locking up and the Gripper grabbed him in the doorway. He lost about a thousand dollars."

"He knows who has money —" I started.

"Let me finish. This guy's still in the hospital. He's going to be OK, but they suspect that the Gripper's turning violent. They say that you just can't tell what he'll do next."

"So what are you going to do?"

"I've got to be in before dark, so Mrs. Anderson is just going to have to put up with that or find someone else to look after Timmy. Anyway, got to go. See you tomorrow."

❂

I was back in my room when Mom opened the door without warning. There I was in the middle of the floor surrounded by puzzle pieces. She must have thought I was working on my homework.

"Oops! I didn't see that," she said, holding up a hand in front of her eyes. "Listen, Tom, about this magic shop work."

"What about it?"

"Two things: Brian and I don't like the idea of you doing it every day of the week. It's too much, sweetie."

"But it'll be finished soon," I protested.

"How soon?"

"A few more days."

"Is that all?"

"Yes, that's all."

"OK. And try to be in before dark, OK? This whole Gripper thing's getting scary."

❖

That night I was lying in bed thinking about Sid and the magic shop. Now that I'd been working there a while, I had to admit that Nick was right, Sid couldn't be earning enough to stay in business. If he had two customers in a day, he'd be lucky. How many kids are into magic, anyway? Sure, he had some makeup kits and some puzzles and games, but you'd never know that from looking at the place. It looked awful. It looked awful from the outside and awful on the inside.

Suddenly, it hit me in a flash. The shop *could* make money. Sid *could* stay in business — if only I could get him to listen to me.

14

The big idea

"Sid," I said. "I *know* it'll work. It'll cost a bit of money, but . . ."

"Tom, I can get more games in," Sid said. "Don't worry about the money. That's no problem for the moment. But the games I have just aren't selling. What makes you think that more games won't just end up collecting dust on the shelves?"

"First, let me fix the front window, OK?"

"If you say so."

The first thing I did was clear out everything. Most of the boxes and packets were so faded from the sun that you couldn't tell what was in them, anyway. Then I cleaned the window inside and out.

Then I got two of the dress dummies from the storeroom. I dressed one of them in Sid's Sigmund the Sorcerer clothing: pin-striped pants, a white ruffled shirt and a bow tie, a long black cape, and his top hat. He had another outfit with a turban and an all-white suit, but I left that in its box in the storeroom.

Then I set up the people-sawing box and put another dummy in it. There was even a wig to make it look more realistic. An old saw in the dummy's hand and two of Sid's old advertising posters on either side finished the job.

Sid went outside and had a good look at it with me.

"It looks great," he said. "You're a consummate artist. I'm afraid I'm just an old one-armed, one-eyed trickster. Making the place look good was never one of my strong points."

As we were standing there, the man and woman from the upstairs apartment came by and then stopped and looked. They were off on their evening walk and had come from the back stairs and then around to the front.

"Giving the place a facelift?" grinned the man.

The woman giggled nervously and brushed her limp hair out of her eyes.

"Dave and Danielle," said Sid, "I'd like you to meet my apprentice, Tom. He's going to make me a rich man, he tells me. Tom, these are my tenants, Dave and Danielle Dinkley. They never promised to make me rich — and they haven't!"

Danielle giggled again and darted a look at Dave. I got the impression that Sid made her nervous. Actually, he had that effect on a lot of people. They didn't understand his sense of humor, I guess.

Dave was sort of macho and didn't look too bright, but he was friendly enough. Danielle seemed nice, too, in a weak, giggly sort of way, but when she shook my hand I was afraid I was going to start her having her baby. I mean, she was so big! She was like a walking time bomb.

I could picture the headline in the *Pen*:

WOMAN HAS BABY ON SIDEWALK
AFTER BOY SHAKES HAND TOO HARD

"Looks good," said Dave, nodding at my window display. Danielle tugged at his arm. She was obviously anxious to keep moving. Before it got too dark, I suppose.

"Lovely people," Sid said as we watched them walk slowly away.

"You'd think they'd be nervous, walking around here at night," I said.

Sid shrugged. "She has to have her exercise, I guess. Exercise for pregnant ladies is all the rage now, isn't it? And she waits until Dave gets home from work. They think he can handle himself well enough for them both."

"But the Gripper's really clever," I said. "And Dave seems a bit dim to me. I don't think he'd be a match for the Gripper at all."

I went on watching Danielle lumbering away. "Let's face it, Danielle couldn't run away from a nasty customer if she was paid to," I added. "I think they're taking a big risk."

Sid paused. "I guess even the Gripper might draw the line at grabbing a pregnant woman like Danielle, Tom," he said after a while. "She's safe, I think."

As we stood there, a car drove by and then turned around and came back. A woman and a young boy got out and looked at the window display. Sid waved me inside and we waited until they came in.

"May I help you, madam?" Sid said. "Sigmund the Sorcerer at your service."

"I didn't even realize this place was here," the woman said. "When did you open?"

"Only five short years ago," Sid said, winking at me. "And it seems we're only now getting ready for business."

Within a few minutes, the boy had picked out one of the most expensive magic sets in the shop, along with a rubber Frankenstein monster mask and a snake.

When they were out of the shop, Sid turned to me. "That's the best sale I've made in weeks! And I owe it to you and your window, Tom."

"That was just the beginning," I said. "You've got to do something about the lighting and the sign's got to be repainted."

"Yeah — it is peeling, I suppose."

"And it doesn't say what it should say," I said.

Sid gave me this very suspicious look.

"What exactly should it say?" he asked.

"It should say 'Sid's Magic and Games.'"

"There you go about games again. I told you —"

"Sid, I'm not talking about jigsaw puzzles. I'm talking about fantasy games, adventure-game books, brain-teaser games, computer games — that's what kids want."

"Now hold on, Tom. Computer games? I don't know anything about computer games. I don't know anything about computers, even. I still don't know what the difference between software and hardware is — except the kind of hardware you buy at the hardware shop."

"Hardware is the machines — computers and printers and all that. Software is the programs — games and stuff."

"Don't bother, Tom. I'm an old dog and you can't teach me new tricks."

"But don't you see," I pleaded, "you don't have to know anything about computers. Well, not at first. They're just in boxes like any other games. We'll tell you which ones to order."

"We?"

"I know a little about them and Nick and Sunny know a lot."

"But there's already a place in town that sells computer games: CompuMart."

"I've thought about that," I said. "But they sell stuff to businesses mostly. They have some games, but only a few. Besides, I suspect kids would much rather come into a place like this and buy."

"Well, you've thought about pretty much everything, Tom. Everything except where I'm going to get the money for all this. I said not to worry about that, but I've been working on it. I don't know if I can stretch to all this. Those computer games are really expensive. Plus there's the new lighting. It's a big gamble."

"Life's not much fun if it isn't a gamble," I reminded him.

Sid let out a long laugh.

"I can see I've got to be careful what I say around here," he said. "OK, give me a few days to think about it. In the meantime, let's forget about the grand schemes and princely riches and get some more cleaning done, shall we?"

"You've got it."

✿

Mrs. Anderson wasn't happy about Sunny and Liz keeping Timmy at home. She said she wasn't sure about Help-for-Hire Inc. and would think about getting someone else to watch him.

She couldn't understand why they couldn't just play nicely with Timmy and have a good time.

"He loves to play," she explained. "He is going through a bit of a rough patch at the moment, but it's all part of growing up. If there is any damage, my husband and I will be happy to pay for it."

As Liz said to me later, the Andersons *had* paid for Nick's new fish. But would they be willing to foot the bill for psychiatric care after Timmy had wrecked our mental health?

15

Problems

The next day — it must have been Thursday because we all delivered the *Pen* that morning — I arrived at Sid's just in time to see the electricians leaving. There were three new fluorescent tubes lighting the aisles and two spotlights in the window. Sid was all smiles when I came in. Jacko sat on the counter beside him.

"Well, I've taken the plunge," Sid said. "I just hope it's the right decision."

"Cost an arm and a leg, Sid," said Jacko.

"Yes, it did, Jacko."

"You've still got the leg to go, Sid."

"That'll be enough, Jacko."

"These'll help pay for it," I said, showing him the jigsaw puzzles I'd managed to sort out.

Of course, we both knew that even if he sold them all it wouldn't come close to paying for even one of the lights.

"I decided it's getting to be sink or swim time," Sid said. "I've been treading water for too long. You made me realize that. By the way, I did some planning. I called some suppliers."

"Of computer games?"

"Yes, and other games. It's all so high-tech these days. Nothing's cheap anymore. When I was a kid, we used to have more fun with old tin cans and bits of wire than you can imagine. These days if kids don't get toys that sing in six languages and stand on their heads, they don't want them."

"You mean, you're really going to get some new games?" I asked excitedly.

"I'll give you a definite maybe on that one, Tom," he said with a wink. He put his hand up Jacko's back.

"Work first, decisions later," said Jacko. "Right, Sid?"

"Right, Jacko."

One problem with the new lights was that now you could see everything much better — so you could see that the floors and shelves were filthy and the paint on the walls and ceiling was peeling.

I went to work clearing shelves and cleaning them with soapy water. When I took a break, Sid showed me how to use a trick magic wand that disappeared and turned into a bunch of colored scarves.

Actually, the scarves came out of the middle of the wand when the wand collapsed. There was a button to push and a spring inside. Once the wand collapsed, you were supposed to put it up your sleeve really quickly. I tried lots of times, but I couldn't do it.

"Practice makes perfect," Sid said. "Don't worry, we'll turn you into another Sigmund the Sorcerer yet."

"Don't hold your breath, Sid," said Jacko.

Just then the Dinkleys came into the shop through the back door.

"Anybody home?" Danielle called, knocking at the side of the door as they came in.

"Enter, enter," said Sid. "What can we do for you?"

"Well, um, it's just . . ." Danielle began. She stopped. "You say it, Dave," she whispered.

Dave stood there for a minute, fidgeting, and then said, "Sorry to say it, Sid, but we have to leave the apartment. We're out a week from Saturday."

Sid looked so shocked. He put his hand over his heart as if to check that it was still beating.

"But why?" he asked.

"It's just that Danielle's about due and we have to start looking for a bigger place."

"A bigger place?" Sid asked. "Isn't there enough room up there? There are two bedrooms. I don't mind the sound of a baby crying, if that's what you're worried about. I know the space is not very fancy, but . . ."

Danielle giggled nervously, brushed her hair back, and put her hand over her stomach. "Oh, it's not the space . . . I mean, there's nothing wrong with the apartment, Mr. Foy," she breathed.

Dave put his arm around her. "To tell the truth, Sid, it's just . . . that I think Danielle's getting a bit . . . you know . . . nervous . . . around here," he said, looking Sid straight in the eye, man to man.

Sid nodded slowly.

"My mother said she'd have us for a while," blurted Danielle. "Till the baby comes. Then we can find a little place of our own. In the country, maybe. Somewhere nice — and quiet."

"Oh, I see," said Sid.

Dave pulled out a small wad of money that he'd already counted.

"This is last month's rent and this month's," he said, holding it out awkwardly. "That should take us up to a week from Saturday." He paused. "Sorry about this, buddy."

When Sid didn't take the money, Dave put it down on the counter. Then he and Danielle left, hand in hand, without saying anything else. Sid didn't say anything else, either, but after they'd gone he started talking about them, and worrying about why they were leaving.

"You don't suppose all the banging around down here disturbed them, do you?" he asked me.

"I don't think so," I said.

"Maybe I was charging them too much for their rent. I thought it was pretty low already, really. Still, I think I'll offer to reduce it even more and see if they'll stay."

"Sid," I said, "I think they just want to move out, that's all. After all, well, you can understand Danielle feeling funny about Raven Hill at the moment, with the Gripper on the loose. Did you hear he mugged three separate people last night? He's never done that before. He's getting greedy."

Sid was silent for a moment. "Danielle wouldn't have had anything to worry about," he said after a moment. "I'm sure of it. It's obvious that people like the Dinkleys don't have money worth taking, anyway. There's no need for them to be scared of the Gripper."

"Well, they obviously are," I said. "Look, Sid, just forget about the Dinkleys. They're boring, anyway. You can rent the apartment to someone else."

"It's not that easy," he muttered. "I don't want just anyone renting above my shop. The Dinkleys were perfect. Perfect." He was almost talking to himself.

"Nice and quiet and not too nosy," said Jacko. "Respectable young couple. Good cover for a villain like you, Sid."

"That'll be enough, Jacko," said Sid absentmindedly. He sighed. "Well, I can't afford to keep the place empty so I guess I'll have to move back in myself."

I remembered what Nick had said about the rent from the apartment keeping the shop going.

"Is this going to affect the . . . the plan?" I asked. "The games and everything?"

He paused. "No," he said slowly at last. "No, it won't affect the plan. I've gone this far. I may as well go the whole way."

"Sink or swim, Sid?" crowed Jacko.

"Sink or swim, Jacko," said Sid.

16

Seeds of doubt

When I got to school on Friday morning, the kids were all talking about another attack by Jack the Gripper. It had happened the night before. This time the victim was Richelle's aunt.

When she drove into her garage after work, he was waiting in there in the dark, so as soon as she got out of the car, he grabbed her and pushed her really hard against the side of the car. Then he snatched her handbag and left her counting while he got away.

She was taken to the hospital with bruises to her head, but they let her go after an hour or two. Of course, she was really rattled. I looked for Richelle to ask her about it, but she hadn't come to school. Some of the kids said that her parents were going to keep her at home till the Gripper was caught.

Liz was worried because it was Richelle's turn, along with Nick, to look after Timmy that afternoon.

There was a new joke going around. "Did you hear about the guy who's going around stealing fish? Jack the Kipper."

The only problem was that half the kids didn't know that kippers were fish.

✿

At lunch, Sunny let me draw a picture of her while she did a chin-up on the branch of a tree in the playground. Of course, this time I drew all of her and not just the head, making it as realistic as possible. The only problem was I was taking too long at it.

"Hurry up, hurry up! My arms are giving out!" Sunny complained. "I thought you were the quickest draw in town!"

I had to finish it with Sunny standing on the ground with her arms up like she was still grasping the branch. Meanwhile, she told me about Timmy's latest drama.

"Elmo and I decided to take him to the *Pen*. We weren't going to take him inside or anything, it was just somewhere to walk to," Sunny explained. "Then, on the way, we heard an ice cream van playing its stupid tune.

"Timmy wanted an ice cream, of course, but he didn't have any money on him. So Elmo told him that the ice cream vans only play that song when they're out of ice cream," Sunny said with a laugh. "Timmy actually believed him, but then he saw people buying stuff. Then Elmo told him that it was winter and you couldn't buy ice cream, you could only order it and they'd deliver it next summer."

"Did he believe it?"

"No. He saw somebody eating one. Then he picked up a rock and said he was going to throw it at a car if we didn't buy him an ice cream."

"So what'd you do?"

"We bought him an ice cream," said Sunny glumly. "What else could we do?"

"The kid is creative," I said. "You have to give him that."

"He was the best he's been so far," Sunny said. "Elmo found a way to tame him. He kept asking him questions about everything. Like he was interviewing him for the *Pen*."

"What kind of questions?"

"Simple ones but not silly ones. Things like, 'Do you think kids should be allowed to eat whatever they want?' and 'How old do you think someone should be to drive a car?' Things like that."

"Did he answer them?"

"He did. That boy is *full* of opinions. Elmo just kept him talking. Simple, huh?"

By now a lot of kids were crowding around me watching me draw. Some of them made stupid comments, but I knew that most of them were impressed. Sunny didn't say anything, but I think she was getting kind of embarrassed.

Anyway, I finished the drawing and I thought it looked pretty good. Sunny didn't. She didn't think it looked anything like her. People hardly ever do think pictures of them *look* like them – not even photographs. Funny, isn't it?

I caught Nick just before the bell ended lunch.

"You've got the little house painter on your own today," I said. "Unless Richelle turns up. What are you going to do?"

"Richelle's here now. I just talked to her. Everything's under control. Today Timmy is going to behave himself like never before."

"Elmo kept him talking and he was OK."

"I know," he said. "I just had a word with him. Timmers and

I have this little understanding: He behaves himself and he gets to keep his front teeth."

"Yeah, sure."

My grin must have irritated Nick. "How's the museum going? Got all the exhibits dusted?" he sneered.

"Have you seen the window?"

"What? You really think cleaning the window's going to do anything?"

"I fixed it up. Have a look. I got some dummies from the back and put Sid's magician clothes on one —"

"Moysten, please."

"Don't laugh. It's really bringing in the customers."

"Pull the other one," he said. "If he sells more than a hundred bucks' worth of that stuff every week, I'll eat that ventriloquist's dummy of his. Come to think of it, I'm surprised *he* hasn't eaten the dummy yet."

"He's got big plans for the place."

"Like what?"

"He wants to start selling lots of different sorts of games — game books and computer games and stuff."

"Really?"

"I suggested it and he liked the idea."

Nick looked at me very seriously.

"Are you sure?" he asked.

"That's what he says."

"Well, maybe he's not as hopeless as I thought he was," Nick said slowly. "But where's he going to get the money?"

I shrugged. I didn't want to talk about Sid's business affairs with Nick.

Nick laughed.

"Hey, he's probably going to raise his tenants' rent," he said. "They won't thank you for your brilliant idea."

"The tenants are moving out," I snapped.

"I'm not surprised," said Nick. "I wouldn't want to be bringing up a baby with a weirdo like Sid hanging around downstairs."

"They're not leaving because of Sid!" I exploded. "They're leaving . . . because of the Gripper. They're obviously scared to walk the streets. It's — it's ridiculous!" I could feel myself going red. "The Gripper's wrecking everyone's lives. Why can't the cops catch him? What's wrong with them?"

Nick stared at me. "Calm down, Moysten," he said. "The Gripper's not your problem. He's not likely to hit you, is he?"

"But why can't they catch him?" I ranted. It was as though once I'd started talking, I couldn't stop. "He can't just disappear into thin air, like they say. No one can run that fast. Someone must see him getting away after these muggings."

Nick shrugged. "Well, no one has, have they? Not so far. He must wear some sort of disguise that he rips off as soon as he's done the robbery. Either that or he's someone you'd never suspect in a million years. Someone from right here in Raven Hill."

I shivered.

Nick looked at me again. "Lighten up, Moysten," he murmured. "You're getting too heated up about this. Just forget about the Gripper. Ever since the cops grabbed you in Memorial Park, you've been acting strange. Cool it."

I knew he was right, of course. I knew I should forget about the Gripper. But I still couldn't help thinking about the conversation afterward. A master of disguise was scary enough. But the idea that the Gripper was someone from right here in Raven Hill, that everyone knew but no one suspected, was even scarier.

All weekend long, I couldn't keep it out of my thoughts.

17

Scary stuff

It was Monday again and Mom was trying to get Adam and Jonathon to finish their breakfasts and get ready for school. There was some drama about money for school photographs. She gave Adam the exact money, but she didn't have the right change for Jonathon. So she handed him a ten-dollar bill.

"Oh, Mom," Jonathon whined. "Ms. Kennedy said we have to have *exactly* the right money. She said 'specially. She said she wasn't a bank lady."

"I don't care what Ms. Kennedy said," Mom said. "Ten dollars is all I've got. I'm not a bank lady, either."

"Aw, Mo-om!"

"Take it or leave it."

And there was even more drama when Jonathon saw that the ten-dollar bill had a corner torn off. Someone had drawn a smiling face in ink near the tear.

"I don't want that one. It's yucky."

"Don't be silly. Money's money."

"Ms. Kennedy won't like it."

I snatched the money away from Mom and said, "Don't you worry, Jonathon. I'll fix it."

I palmed the money off into the other hand and pretended to put it in my mouth. Then I chewed and chewed and then swallowed and gulped. Adam and Jonathon were fascinated. You could see from their faces that they really thought I'd swallowed it.

"There," I said. "It's gone. No more yucky ten-dollar bill."

Brian looked up from his breakfast cereal.

"Don't teach them to put money in their mouths," he said. "It's filthy. You're setting a bad example."

"I didn't really put it in my mouth," I whispered.

"I know that," he said. "But they will."

The man is a moron.

"I want it! Give it back!" Jonathon squealed.

"It's all gone," I said, taking it out of my pocket. "But I've got another one."

Jonathon took it and unfolded it.

"Aw, that's the same ten dollars," he yelled. "I can tell. It's got that face on it."

"Oh, didn't you know?" I said. "That's the way they're making all ten-dollar bills now."

"Liar! Liar! Liar!" Adam shrieked, banging his spoon on his bowl in excitement. "Do it again, Tom! Again!"

Anyway, it had worked. Jonathon agreed to take the money.

As I was going out the door, Mom said, "Thanks, Tom. And remember we're visiting Mrs. Moysten in the hospital tonight."

Mrs. Moysten is my grandmother — Dad's mother. For some reason, Mom always calls her Mrs. Moysten when Brian's around. She seems kind of embarrassed that they're still friends even though Mom and Dad split up. Anyway, Grandma just had an eye operation and Mom thought we should both go and see her.

"No problemo," I said.

"Make sure you finish up at the magic shop in time to meet me at six o'clock by the bank. The usual place. Brian's using the car so we'll take the bus over."

"Sure."

"And get some flowers from Grace's Flower Shop on the way. I'll pay you back."

"What kind of flowers?"

"Something cheery. Tell Grace they're for your grandmother. She'll know."

○

At school I heard the bad news about Richelle and Nick's Friday Timmy-minding. They'd tried Elmo's talking technique and it had worked — at first. They'd walked Timmy all around the place, talking, till their legs were nearly dropping off. And then they stopped at Richelle's house.

Richelle's sister was at home and so was her mother. How could he get into trouble with four people watching him? Well, Nick and Richelle started watching TV and everyone else was busy with something. The next thing anybody knew, there were leaves all over the floor. Timmy had picked every leaf off every potted plant in the house!

"It's winter," he said. "The leaves fall on the ground."

As his mother said, he is a creative little person.

○

When I got to the shop in the afternoon, I found Sid in a cheery mood. He had his artificial arm on and was making Jacko talk quite a bit. He seemed to have recovered from his disappointment at losing his tenants at the end of the week. I thought how stupid I'd been to let Nick's sneers about him worry me.

Sid said that he'd sold a lot of stuff over the weekend thanks to my window. He reckoned that since it was done he was getting four times as many customers as before. That's what he said.

But only a couple of people came into the shop while I was working. Was he telling the truth about all the extra customers? *He must be*, I thought. *Why would he lie?*

The storeroom was cleared out now and the trash had been taken away over the weekend. I pulled down some more of the magic sets that Timmy had scrambled and spread them out on the floor. Then I started putting them back together again. It wasn't such a hard job and after about an hour I had ten complete sets ready to be taped up and sold.

Somehow, the dust was really getting to me today. I kept sneezing and my eyes were watering.

"Take a break!" Sid called out. "I don't want to get the Help-for-Hire union on me for working you too hard."

"I've just got a few more sets to go," I said.

"Well, for heaven's sake, stop sneezing," he said. "Are you coming down with something?"

"It's the dust," I said. "I'll be OK in a little while."

"Good. When you've got a minute, come here. I want to cut off your finger."

I wondered if I'd heard him right.

"The kid's got another egg in his ear, Sid," said Jacko's voice.

"No, I heard," I called. "I'm on my way."

On the counter in front of Sid with Jacko was a big pile of money — most of it probably the two months' rent money he'd gotten from the Dinkleys. But there was also a small metal gadget. I'd never seen anything like it before.

"What's that?" I asked.

"You know those things that cut the ends off expensive cigars? The things with a razor blade in them and you put the cigar in and *bam!* you hit it with your fist and it slices the end of the cigar off?"

I'd never heard of anything like that.

"Not really," I said.

"The boy doesn't smoke cigars, Sid," said Jacko.

"I didn't imagine he did, Jacko," said Sid.

"So what's the point, Sid?"

"I'm explaining this gizmo to him, Jacko. It's like a cigar cutter. Here, Tom, put your finger in."

I stuck out my finger and brought it close to the hole.

"Watch it," warned Jacko. "That thing's sharp!"

What am I doing? I thought. *This guy is about to cut off my finger and I'm letting him do it!*

Sid grabbed my hand gently in his and pushed my finger into the hole as far as it would go.

"There now," he said, raising his fist in the air to hit the lever. "Off it comes!"

Suddenly, he stopped.

"No," he said, pulling out a carrot from under the counter. "Maybe we'd better try it out on this first, just to make sure it's working."

I pulled out my finger and he put the carrot in. Then he pounded the top of the cutter with his fist and the carrot fell into two neat pieces.

"Works all right, Sid," said Jacko.

"Yup," said Sid. "It works on carrots, anyway. Now let's give it the finger test."

I hesitated.

"What's wrong, Tom?" he asked.

"I — I don't know," I said.

"He's scared to death, if you ask me, Sid," said Jacko. "Doesn't trust you."

"Don't you trust old Sigmund the Sorcerer, Tom? I thought you were the sorcerer's apprentice!"

"Well —"

"I wouldn't trust him, either," said Jacko.

Slowly, I put my finger into the cutting hole. In a flash, Sid's artificial hand had grabbed my wrist, jamming the finger in place. He raised his fist in the air again.

"No!" I yelled, screwing my eyes shut.

Sid's fist pounded the top of the cutter with a crash. In that terrifying moment, I could feel the cold steel of the blade and I knew that my finger was lying in a pool of blood on the counter.

I opened my eyes to see Sid's face. For a minute, I didn't

move. I was still sure my finger had been sliced in two. Then I pulled it slowly out of the cutter.

My finger was OK. There was only a slight red line across the top where the metal had touched it.

"Bad luck, Sid," said Jacko.

"I guess I'd better get the blade sharpened," Sid laughed. "That thing wouldn't slice anything but carrots. Hey, are you all right?"

I don't know if it was the sneezing or the fear but I rocked back on my heels and felt like I was going to faint.

"I'm OK," I said.

"It's just a trick," Sid said. "If I'd have known it was going to affect you that way —"

"I'm OK," I said again.

"Tom, you've been working too hard. You're jumpy as a cat. I want you to take a day off, all right? I don't want you to come in tomorrow. You need more time to relax and to get some studying done. I'll pay you just the same —"

"No way."

"I owe it to you for all your good suggestions. You've made a lot of money for me."

I knew I'd had no reason to be scared, but that finger-cutting business had kind of given me the creeps. Besides, Sid was just the last in a long line of people to say I was being jumpy and strange lately. I found I really liked the idea of having a day off.

"All right. Thanks," I said.

"And would you mind closing up tonight? I've left my car at the service station and I have to go over to pick it up before it closes."

I looked at the stack of money on the counter.

"Are you going to leave all that money here?" I asked.

"I'll put it in the lockbox. It'll be OK. No one ever breaks in here. I'm just too busy to put it in the bank."

"I'll deposit it for you on my way home," I said. "You just fill out one of those slips and put it in an envelope."

"You're a treasure, Tom."

Sid put the money in an envelope, dropped it in the box, and then left the shop.

I stayed on, pleased that I'd be able to help, but without any idea of what was to come.

18

The attack

Wouldn't you know it? Just when I was going to close the shop, these kids came in with their mother and they wanted to play with everything.

It was getting close to six and I was trying to hurry them out, but they just kept looking at things. I didn't want to be rude, of course. They were Sid's customers, not mine.

Finally, they bought two jigsaw puzzles and an expensive magic set. It was a great sale. I couldn't wait to tell Sid about it.

At five minutes to six, I put the envelope into my schoolbag, locked the door, and sprinted down the street to where I was supposed to meet Mom.

Needless to say, I was late. And Mom wasn't impressed.

"Sorry," I panted. "I was closing up and there was a customer."

"Where are the flowers?"

The flowers! I'd completely forgotten the flowers!

"I'll get them now," I said.

"Grace has probably closed by now. She closes at six and it's already ten past."

"I'll see," I said, throwing my bag down at her feet. "Keep an eye on that. I'll be right back."

I raced off around the corner and up a couple of blocks. The flower shop was dark, but Grace was outside hosing down the sidewalk.

"I need some flowers." I begged. "It's urgent!"

Grace laughed.

"I haven't got much left," she warned. But she opened the door of the shop and let me go in. I grabbed a bunch of little pink rosebuds, plunked down the money, and was out the door shouting my thanks in a minute.

It was when I was running back along the dark street with the flowers in my hand that I sensed that something was wrong. I don't know why, but I just had this feeling. Then I came around the corner and Mom was nowhere in sight. My heart skipped a beat.

I peered around in the darkness. Then I saw her — lying on the ground by the wall.

"Mom!"

I heard her groan before I reached her.

"Mom!"

"I'm all right," she croaked. She began struggling to get up, holding her hand to her throat.

"Was it . . . ? Did you . . . ?" I stammered, trying to help her.

"The phone — over there . . . quickly! Dial nine-one-one . . ."

Sure enough, it had been the Gripper. The police were there in a flash, but it didn't do much good. As usual, the Gripper had gotten clean away. Nobody nearby had seen anyone running or anyone acting suspiciously.

While Mom was talking to the police, her right eye became more and more swollen until it was completely closed.

"We'll take you to the hospital," one of the police officers said.

"No! No, thank you," Mom whispered, holding on to my hand. "It's OK, really. I just want to get home and cancel my credit cards."

"The Gripper doesn't use stolen credit cards. If he did, we'd've caught him by now," the officer said. "It's up to you, ma'am, but I'd get the eye looked at. Now, could you just briefly go over what you told us one last time?"

"As I said, I was waiting here for Tom," Mom began wearily. "He's been working in the afternoons at Sid's Magic Shop. He arrived, and then ran back to buy some flowers for his grandmother."

I stood by helplessly, listening. If only I hadn't forgotten the flowers! If only I hadn't left Mom alone like that. If only . . .

"I didn't hear the Gripper coming up behind me," Mom said. "I didn't hear a thing. Before I knew it, his arm went around my throat. He was strong. Really strong. He sort of jerked my head back so I nearly choked. And there was this thing poking in my back. A gun, maybe."

I felt her hand tighten on mine.

"He grabbed my bag," she went on. "He told me not to move or look at him and to count to fifty. Just when he let go, I turned my head sideways for a second. I didn't mean to. It was just automatic. That's when he hit me and I fell down."

"So you must have seen him when you turned," the police officer said.

"Not properly." Mom shuddered. "I got just a glimpse before he hit me and — it was horrible!"

"Horrible? In what way?"

"I can't describe it." Mom shuddered again. "He was frightfully pale, and snarling at me. And he'd been — hurt." She paused.

"Hurt?" urged the officer.

"I think he had a deep cut on his forehead running down over his eye, and some other scars, too," Mom said. "It was just horrible. Nightmarish." She stopped again, and swallowed. "Sorry," she said, "I'm being silly. It can't have been as bad as that."

"Shock can play tricks on our memories," said the officer, closing his notebook. "Don't worry about it anymore now, ma'am. We'll call on you again in the morning, when you've had a chance to calm down."

The police offered to give us a lift home. It was only then that I looked around for my schoolbag.

"Hey! Where's my bag?" I yelled.

"He must have taken it," Mom said helplessly. "I didn't notice."

"Oh, no!" I cried. "It had a whole lot of Sid's money in it. I was going to deposit it at the bank for him."

My stomach knotted up. I couldn't believe it! I looked around again, desperately, but the bag was gone.

"How much money?" the policeman asked. "Not so much, surely. Old Sid doesn't exactly make a fortune out of that shop, by the look of it."

"I don't know exactly what was there," I said. "But there was an awful lot. A whole wad of it. Oh, no! What am I going to do? I'll have to tell him!"

"You go home with your mother," said the police officer. "Sid lives at the trailer park these days, doesn't he? He's a harmless old guy, but we keep an eye on him all the same, if you know what I mean. We'll go out there and see him. We'll tell him. Just leave it to us."

I was glad to. I didn't want to see Sid's face when he found out what had happened. His profits *and* his rent money — gone with the Gripper. And all because of me!

19

The face

Brian was really upset, of course. He wanted Mom to go to the hospital, too, but she wouldn't hear of it. She phoned Grandma to say that we weren't coming to visit because she wasn't feeling well. She didn't tell the whole story so as not to worry her.

Jonathon listened to everything and then told us proudly about his own *personal* robbery.

"I didn't get my school photos," he said brightly.

Of course, nobody was particularly interested what with Brian checking out Mom's black eye and me worrying about Sid.

"Guess what happened?" Jonathon asked. "Guess why I didn't get my photos?"

"The camera broke when they took a picture of you," I said.

"No," he said. "Timmy stole the money."

"What?! Why that little — !"

"He took the envelope out of my bag."

"Did you see him do it?"

"No. But he did it," Jonathon said firmly. "He always steals stuff."

"Did you tell your teacher?" Brian asked Jonathon.

"Yes."

"And what did she say?"

"She said nobody saw Timmy take the money. So she said maybe someone else took it."

While all this was going on, I had a bright idea.

"Mom," I said, "you know those police artists' drawings? The ones they draw from witnesses' descriptions? To help identify criminals?"

"What about them?"

"You tell me what the Gripper looked like and I'll draw a picture!"

"I don't think I'm remembering him properly, Tom," Mom said. "I was so scared and shocked. There was only a glance. And what I thought I saw was so . . . weird."

"I know, you said that," I said. "But let's give it a shot, OK?"

I'll say this for Mom: Even though she was still shaken up from the robbery, she was a good sport. I did sketch after sketch of the Gripper's face just from her saying things like, "No, the nose was flatter" and "The scar is longer and closer to his eyebrows."

It was the most hideous face I'd ever seen. We were all sure that if he lived in Raven Hill we'd have noticed him, and remembered.

And yet, I did remember the face. I'd seen it before, maybe a long time ago. Or was it a face from a TV show or a magazine? Somewhere the face had crept quietly into my memory. And now I knew it wouldn't go away until the mystery of the Gripper was solved.

✿

All I could think about that night was the police breaking the news to Sid. This would certainly put him out of business. I felt so guilty. If only I'd let him leave the money in the shop it would still be safe.

At school the next day, I was a major celebrity. Everybody wanted to know about the robbery. I told the Help-for-Hire gang, but then I got tired of going over the same old story to everyone else. And I didn't tell anyone about Sid's money.

I thought of calling him, but I couldn't bring myself to do it. I wouldn't have to see him that afternoon, but sooner or later, I was going to have to face the music.

Liz caught up to me in the hallway.

"Big problems," she said. "Nick and Richelle say they won't look after Timmy again."

"You can hardly blame them, can you?"

"I know, but his parents are out till five-thirty. I can't contact them."

"So?"

"So someone's got to pick him up from school."

"Can't Nick and Richelle just take him straight to his house and stay there with him?"

"Tom, you don't understand: Richelle wants to kill him — and so does Nick. They've absolutely refused. They say they'll quit Help-for-Hire rather than deal with him."

"How about Sunny and Elmo?" I said. "They're the only ones who can handle the kid."

"Elmo and I had him yesterday and he was OK. We spent two hours talking to him. You just can't ignore him, that's all.

You have to be prepared to spend two hours talking to him and playing with him."

"Well, then you can do it again today," I said. "Simple."

"It's Tuesday. Elmo's busy helping his father at the *Pen*. I have to meet my mom at four-thirty to go shopping. Sunny's supposed to be walking the dog today. That's only an hour, so I can do that instead of her and she can take Timmy. But she can't do it alone."

She paused. I waited. I knew what was coming.

"Nick said you're not working at the shop today," she said casually, at last.

"Oh, no, you don't, Liz!" I said. "I never wanted to look after the kid in the first place! I warned you."

"It's good money."

"I don't care how much it is. Do you realize that little monster stole ten dollars from my brother?"

"Sunny knows how to handle him, believe me," Liz said. She began backing away. "Just meet her at his school at three-thirty," she added. "Bye!" She started running while I still had my mouth open to protest. "Thanks, Tom, you're a prince," she called back over her shoulder.

"Make that a pushover," I grumbled to myself. "OK, I'll do it. But I won't like it."

❂

Sunny and I picked up Timmy from school and walked him back to his apartment. Mrs. Anderson had left the key under a potted plant so we could let ourselves in.

From Timmy's place, I could see the back of the row of shops where Sid's place was. Next door to him was an empty building with a broken-down old garage behind it. Vines were growing all over the garage doors. The place was dark, abandoned for years after the shop had gone out of business. I wondered if Sid's would be the same someday.

For the moment, the new bright lights were on in the magic shop, lighting the alley behind.

"That's the crazy man," Timmy said, pointing at the shop. "He's crazy!"

I kept thinking about going over and talking to Sid. Maybe I should go over that evening after watching the little monster. I couldn't leave it till the next day. Chances were Sid wouldn't want to see me ever again, anyway. Who could blame him?

Sunny had this really good way with Timmy. She'd talk to him right on his level like she was his age. I was hopeless. I'd think of a question like, "What do you want to be when you grow up?" and he'd say, "I don't know. That's stupid!" I guess I just didn't have the knack.

Then I had a better idea. I pulled out a handkerchief and poked it down into my fist the way Sid had taught me. Then I blew on it and opened my hand and it was gone.

"How did you do that?!" Timmy squealed.

"Magic, my boy, magic."

"How? How? How?"

He loved it. I did it again and again.

Then I pulled a quarter out of his ear and he loved that one, too. And I made it disappear.

"I'll show you how to do it," I said, and I did it in slow

motion, showing him how I pretended to put it in one hand but really put it in the other.

"You're not bad," Sunny said. "I'm impressed."

"Years of practice," I said.

That's when Timmy decided to do it himself. I told him to use his own coin. (Why should I let the kid rip me off?) He searched his pockets and came up with a ten-dollar bill. Not just any ten-dollar bill, though. It was Jonathon's ten-dollar bill!

"Hey!" I said grabbing it out of his hand. "Where did you get that?"

Timmy got really angry and tried to grab it back.

"What are you doing?" Sunny said in surprise.

"Look at this," I said, showing her the bill. "See that torn corner and the face? I've seen this bill before. I happen to know who it belongs to." I turned to Timmy. "Don't you *ever* take someone else's money again," I said to him.

He looked very embarrassed and didn't say anything when I put the bill in my pocket.

20

Facing the music

I thought of telling Timmy's parents about the ten dollars, but in the end I didn't. I'd gotten it back, after all. Why complicate things? It was bad enough that they were up for the price of seven tropical fish and about fifteen potted plants.

I told Sunny about Sid's lost money and she stopped by the magic shop with me. I told her she didn't have to, but I was really glad she did.

Sid was there, getting ready to close the shop.

"Is your mother all right?" he said as soon as he saw me.

So the police *had* spoken to him, like they said they would.

"She's just kind of shaken, that's all," I said. "She's got a black eye."

He shook his head. "I couldn't believe it when the cops told me," he said. "Your mother!" He shook his head again. "It's a terrible thing, all these robberies. It's not safe to walk the streets anymore."

"Sid?" I began.

"Yes, Tom?"

"You know that money I was going to deposit last night?"

"The police told me," he said. "The Gripper got it. Never mind. It wasn't your fault."

He was so calm! I couldn't believe it.

"I'll pay you back," I mumbled, feeling my cheeks get hot.

"Big spender!" squawked Jacko, from a shadowy corner.

Sid grinned. "How could you do that? Be sensible, Tom. Let's just chalk it up to experience."

"Well, I don't have the money now," I said, "but I'll earn it. I'll pay it off bit by bit. I promise."

Sid laughed aloud this time.

"That's very kind of you," he said, "but I couldn't expect you to do that. No, it was my decision to let you take the money. I was responsible for what happened."

"But, Sid —"

"No arguments, Tom. This is your day off, so let's not discuss it anymore. Off you go. I'll see you tomorrow."

"You're crazy, Sid!" said Jacko.

"That'll be enough, Jacko!"

"Sorry, Sid!"

❈

Sunny and I stopped at a café up the street and I bought a couple of milk shakes with the torn ten-dollar bill. I could pay Mom back later.

We sat at a table outside, on the sidewalk, drinking the milk shakes, and then I saw Danielle and Dave walking toward us, arm in arm. Danielle saw me, and said something to Dave. She seemed to be trying to persuade him to do something, because at first he shook his head, and then shrugged his shoulders. I wondered what was up.

They stopped at our table. "Not working at the shop today, Tom?" said Dave in a casual sort of way. "Finished the job already?"

"No," I said. "I just have the afternoon off."

I thought they looked disappointed. "Why?" I said. "Is there a problem?"

They both shook their heads violently. "Oh, no! No!" said Dave, looking embarrassed. "We were just — you know, wondering."

Danielle nudged him.

He glanced at Sunny and then back at me. "We just thought — you know — that shop doesn't seem — you know — the best sort of place for a kid to be spending all that time," he babbled. "That's all we thought."

"It's OK," I said coldly. Why was everyone against me? I fumed. Why was everyone always trying to stop me from doing things I wanted to do?

"Oh. Right." Dave glanced at Danielle. "Well, we'd better be off," he said. "Give the old girl her exercise."

"Dave!" smiled Danielle. "You're awful!"

They waved and went on, moving carefully past the tables so Danielle's big stomach wouldn't bash into anything.

"It's good she likes to exercise," Sunny said. "Mom says too many women get out of shape when they're going to have a baby. They seem quite nice."

"They're boring. But still, I wish they weren't leaving the apartment," I said. "Sid really needs that money, I know he does."

"Do you feel better now that you've talked to him?"

"I guess so," I said. "I still feel really bad, though. He was so *nice* about it."

Sunny slurped the last of her milk shake.

"It was a bit weird, wasn't it?" she said.

"What was?"

"Just what you said. He's taken losing the money so well. Nobody loses that much money and stays calm about it. The average person would go out of their mind."

"Sid's not your average person," I said.

"That's for sure," said Sunny. She looked thoughtfully at me.

✿

In my dreams that night, I was walking alone through an old warehouse. There was water dripping onto the floor from above. Where was it coming from? I found an old staircase and went up. There in the middle of a huge empty room was a plastic bucket like the one I'd been using to clean the magic shop. I came up to it slowly and looked inside. There, in a pool of blood, was the Gripper's face looking up at me.

That face! I let out an ear-piercing scream.

"Are you all right, darling?"

It was Mom, sitting on the edge of my bed, running her fingers through my sweaty hair.

"I'm OK," I mumbled. "Just a bad dream."

"It's the Gripper, isn't it?" she said. She shivered. "I've been having nightmares myself. But, really, we should try to forget him, darling."

"I'm all right, Mom. Don't worry."

"Tom?"

"Yes?"

"From now on, could you leave the magic shop in plenty of time to get home before dark?"

"Sure."

○

When I got to the shop on Wednesday, Sid was in an even better mood than he'd been the night before. But there was something really strange about him — like he was really excited about something, something he didn't want to tell me about. I hadn't ever seen him like this. And Jacko was jokier than ever.

"There'll be some more cleaning work when Dave and Danielle leave next Saturday, Tom," he said. "Got to get the apartment ready for a new tenant — namely, me."

"And me, Sid," said Jacko.

"Of course, Jacko. I do apologize."

"Aren't you even going to *try* to find someone to rent it?" I said.

"Oh, no. I'm looking forward to moving in again. Now that the shop's on its feet I want to be right where the action is. I want to keep an eye on things. Especially with the new plan in operation."

Sid looked at me with a twinkle in his eye.

"What plan?" I asked.

"*Your* plan, Tom," he said. "How soon you forget! The computer games and all that other mumbo-jumbo stuff."

"Are you serious?"

"No! He's crazy!" Jacko chimed in.

"Take no notice of him," Sid said. "Have a look in the storeroom."

Sure enough, there in the back were cartons and cartons of new games, books — and even a computer!

"Of course, you'll have to help me get set up," Sid said. "I'm relying on you."

I couldn't believe my eyes.

"How did you do this?" I asked.

"You mean where did I get the money?"

"Well, yes."

"If I told you that Sigmund the Sorcerer just made it appear out of thin air, would you believe me?" Sid laughed. "Or don't you really believe in magic?"

"Well, not when it comes to money," I said.

"The kid's not as silly as he looks, Sid," said Jacko.

"That'll be enough, Jacko."

"Sorry, Sid."

"Come on, then," Sid grinned at me. "What are you waiting for? There's a computer to set up and lots of stock to put out on the shelves. There's an old dog here that wants to learn some new tricks! Hop to it! Let's go!"

It was like a dream come true. In an hour we had a whole aisle stocked with the new games and I'd even managed to set up the computer and show Sid how to run a demo of one of the games, Space Gauntlet III.

A few customers came in, bought things, and left again. One of them even bought a computer game. The next time the door screamed and laughed, it was Mom. She'd brought Adam and Jonathon along with her.

Jonathon's eyes lit up when he saw the computer, and he started playing with it right away.

"I'm Grace Murphy, Tom's mother," Mom said to Sid. "I just thought I'd see how things were going."

"I was sorry to hear about your . . . your accident," Sid said, looking at Mom's black eye.

"I'll be OK in a few days. It's the shock of the thing," Mom said. "*I'm* sorry you had to lose *your* money."

"Don't be, dear lady. It was just one of those things. You win a few and you lose a few."

"You lost an arm," said Jacko. "When are you going to win one, Sid?"

Adam and Jonathon stared at him, openmouthed.

"That'll be enough, Jacko!"

"Sorry, Sid."

Mom smiled. "Tom," she said, turning to me, "have you shown Mr. Foy the sketch you made of the Gripper?"

Sid jumped. "You actually *saw* him?" he asked me.

"Mom did," I said. "I just sketched him from Mom's description. It really doesn't look like anything."

I took the drawing out of my bag and showed it to Sid. Maybe I imagined it, but he looked shocked. He turned to me.

"If I were you," he said, "I'd keep that hidden. Don't show it around."

"Do you know who it is?"

"No, I don't. But it's pretty obvious that this guy doesn't want anyone to see him. He may not know you saw him, Mrs.

Murphy. I wouldn't show it around if I were you. Have the police seen it?"

"No," I said.

"Good. My advice would be to keep it to yourself. The fewer people who know about it, the better."

21

A secret place

"Pete had his money stolen at school," Jonathon said.

"Pete who?" I asked.

"Pete Free."

Liz's little brother. That miniature crook Timmy had come out of retirement already!

"Luckily, Jonathon lent Pete some money for lunch," Mom said. "Right, Jonno?"

"I found two dollars in my bag," Jonathon said proudly. "I think it was left over from the photo money."

"What are you talking about?" I asked.

"The photo money envelope must have torn," he said. "Some money fell out. So Timmy didn't get it all. Stinks!"

"Now, wait a minute. What's this about two dollars? You didn't have any singles. You had a ten-dollar bill," I said, remembering the money I'd taken back from Timmy.

"No, he didn't," Mom said.

"But I saw it," I said. "A ten-dollar bill. It was torn. It had a little face on it."

"No," Mom said. "I took that one back. Brian found the right money for Jonathon to take in the end."

"What happened to the ten-dollar bill?"

"I put it back in my bag. I guess the Gripper got it."

The Gripper? If the Gripper got it, how had Timmy ended up with it? Timmy might be a real pain, but he couldn't possibly be the Gripper!

"Listen, Tom," Mom said. "I've got to get back and start dinner. Do you want me to send Brian down to pick you up?"

"No. Thanks, anyway. I'll get back before dark."

"Promise?"

"Promise."

❁

Sid let me go about fifteen minutes early. But I had to know where Timmy had gotten that ten-dollar bill, so I ducked around to the back to wait for Liz and Sunny to bring Timmy home.

I watched Danielle and Dave come down the back stairs at Sid's and out into the alley, starting off on their evening walk.

They noticed me and stared. I suppose I must have looked odd, hanging around like that. But then Dave grinned and Danielle gave me a friendly wave. I waved back and they walked on, with Danielle clinging to Dave's arm. I wondered if he really would be a match for the Gripper. He was strong, but he wasn't too bright. And Danielle certainly wouldn't be. Not in her condition. I hoped Sid was right when he said they'd be safe.

✿

The wait was longer than I expected. The sun had disappeared behind the row of apartments and I knew Mom would be worrying about me by now.

Finally, Sunny and Timmy came along. Liz wasn't with them.

"She had to go home," Sunny explained, "so I brought him back on my own. He's actually being a good kid, aren't you, Timmy?"

"Yup," said Timmy.

"Timmy," I said, kneeling down to be on his level, "I have a very important question to ask you."

The kid looked at me very suspiciously.

"Remember the ten dollars I took from you?" I said. "I'd like you to tell me where you got it."

"What is this about?" Sunny asked. "Didn't he get it at school?"

"I don't think so," I said. "Tell me, Tim."

Timmy shook his head from side to side.

"Please," I pleaded.

Timmy just shook his head again.

"I'll tell you what," I said, getting a box out of my pocket. "This is itching powder. Put it down someone's shirt and they'll itch like crazy. Think of all the fun you can have with it."

He grabbed for it and I pulled it back, out of reach.

"Not so fast," I said. "You tell me where you got the ten dollars and then I'll give it to you."

"Promise?"

"Cross my heart and hope to die. How about it?"

"Over there," Timmy said, pointing across the alley.

He led us to the old garage beside the backyard of the magic shop. He pulled the weeds and ivy aside and wiggled through a small space between the double doors.

"Hey! Where'd you go? Come out of there!" I whispered.

Sunny and I squeezed through the gap and into the garage. It was getting dark now and it was even darker inside. Only the light from Sid's shop next door, streaming through the cracks in the boards, showed us the piles of old broken furniture and other things stacked around the walls.

In the corner, Timmy was kneeling over a black plastic bag. He opened the top so that we could see inside.

"Tom!" Sunny exclaimed. "It's full of handbags and wallets!"

We started looking through the bag. There were dozens of bags and wallets there. Everything was still in them — drivers' licenses, credit cards, all sorts of junk. Everything but the money. On top was my schoolbag and Mom's handbag. Sure enough, Mom's money was missing and so was Sid's rent money.

Sunny and I looked at each other.

"It's the Gripper's stuff, isn't it?" Sunny said.

"You're not wrong," I answered. "Was the ten dollars in here?" I asked Timmy.

"Over there," he said, pointing to the ground.

"He must have dropped it," Sunny said. "Or maybe he didn't want it because it was marked. Maybe he thought he'd be caught if he tried to spend it."

I stood there looking at it for a minute, thinking. Trying to piece things together.

Who was he, this man with the horrible face? He must live nearby. The shop next to Sid's was abandoned, but what if the Gripper had been camping in there? No one would know. And this garage would be a perfect dumping ground for the evidence of his robberies. No one would ever look in here. No one except a nosy, naughty little kid.

I went to look at the door that led into the abandoned shop's backyard. It was bolted shut. And the bolt was rusty and covered in spiderwebs.

"Let's get out of here!" Sunny whispered. "Call the police!"

"Just a minute. There's something I can't understand."

"What?"

"The Gripper must be very skinny to get into this place. Those doors, front and back, haven't been opened in years. And I only just made it through that gap that leads out to the alley. If the Gripper's been squeezing through that over and over again, the ivy would be all smashed up, no doubt about it."

Timmy stood up and pointed to the side wall. There was a sheet of plywood propped up against it. I grabbed it and slid it sideways along the ground. There in the wall behind was a big hole — big enough for anyone to climb through. Light streamed through it from the back of the magic shop.

"That's it!" Sunny whispered. "That's how he gets in! First he gets into Sid's backyard and then he just climbs through."

Suddenly, it struck me like a thunderbolt. The face! The Gripper's face. No wonder Mom had called it nightmarish and horrible! It was one of those rubber masks from the magic shop.

My mind was in a whirl. The Gripper! Someone everyone knew but no one would suspect in a million years, Nick had said. Someone who needed money, and didn't know how else to get it, Brian had said.

The pieces fell into place like a horrible jigsaw. The Gripper. Someone who could disguise his voice. Someone who could disappear like magic. Someone with one strong arm to catch his victims around the throat, and something hard to press against their backs. Like a gun — or a metal hand . . .

I made a choking sound.

Outside, something moved.

"What was that?" Sunny whispered.

Then, suddenly, there he was, crouching by the hole looking in, blocking out the light.

"Sid!" I yelled. "Sid!"

He grabbed the piece of plywood in his hand and threw it to the side, his body now halfway through the hole.

Timmy screamed and we ran for the doors, but a powerful arm shot out, punching me in the back of the head. A white flash of pain shot through my skull as I went crashing over a barrel and into a pile of flowerpots, sending them flying in all directions.

"Run, Sunny! Timmy! Get the cops!" I screamed.

But Sunny was spinning around. Then she was leaping, twisting, her feet crashing into the man's stomach. He grunted, doubled over. And Sunny's leg was flashing forward, hitting him squarely under the chin and sending him crashing to the ground.

It was only when he lay there, unconscious on the ground, that we saw who it really was.

Dave. I couldn't believe my eyes. Stupid, macho Dave Dinkley was the Gripper!

"Let's get out of here!" I screamed, crawling over to Sunny and struggling to my feet.

"No, you don't!"

A hard arm grabbed me around the throat as the new voice growled the words.

Even as I struggled against the strangling grip and heard Sunny's gasping cries as she fought our attacker, my mind registered the shock.

Danielle!

Her arms were like iron bands. She had us both, one on each side, and we gasped for breath as she squeezed tighter and tighter. I tried kicking at her legs, but it was no use. In terror I felt myself drifting into unconsciousness.

"Help!" I tried to scream, but nothing more than a soft croak came out.

Suddenly, Danielle gave a huff of surprise. Then she swore. Her strangling grip around our necks loosened. And the next moment, she was writhing on the ground with Timmy standing over her, emptying the last of the box of itching powder all over her body.

"I'll get you for this!" Danielle screamed, frantically tearing at her clothes and rubbing at her legs and arms and neck. "You . . . !"

Sunny was on her feet in a second, grabbing ropes and rags from the garage floor, looping them around the struggling Danielle's feet and hands, and pulling them tight.

I tried to do the same thing with Dave. He was stirring. My hands were shaking as I fumbled with the knots. The ropes and rags were old. *How long would they hold?* I thought. *Long enough for us to get away? For us to get through the gap in the door, across the dark alley, disappear into Timmy's apartment where they couldn't find us? Long enough for . . . ?*

"Hey! Look at this!" Sunny gasped.

There in the half-light we saw it, on Danielle's stomach, where her smock had bunched up as she writhed and struggled. It was hard and round, like a bowl or the shell of a big turtle, strapped around the woman's body. Sunny grabbed it and pulled it away and when she did, a handbag, a toy gun, and a hideous rubber mask fell out.

"She's not pregnant at all!" Sunny yelled. "She just used her false stomach to carry the loot. No wonder the Gripper always got away so fast! Who'd suspect a pregnant woman and her husband? And even if they did, the stolen stuff was completely hidden."

Danielle was baring her teeth at us, growling with rage, pulling at the ropes that bound her.

"You'll be sorry," she spat at me. "I thought you were up to something, hanging around in the alley. I knew you'd be trouble, poking around. When I catch you . . ."

She was getting loose! I grabbed Sunny's hand and Timmy's shirt and started hurrying them toward the gap in the door.

But Dave had gotten to his knees now. He was ripping and tearing with his teeth at the rags on his wrists. In one minute . . . half a minute . . .

"This is the police! Don't anybody in there move! Stay right where you are!" barked a voice from the magic shop's backyard.

"In there, Lieutenant! Cover me!" shouted another voice from the alley.

Sirens filled the air.

The police! I was never so relieved in all my life!

The police went on barking orders and shouting to one another. There must have been six of them out there at least, I figured. More than enough to beat Dave and Danielle.

"Lie flat on the floor, facedown, you two. Send the children out!" the first voice ordered. "One at a time. And no funny business or we'll come in firing!"

At that, Danielle and Dave stopped struggling and lay back. They knew when they were beaten.

Shaking like a leaf, I crawled out after Timmy into the magic shop's backyard. Sunny came after me.

We stood up and looked around for the police team.

And saw an empty yard full of voices — and Sid!

22

Help-for-Hire strikes again!

The police did arrive soon after that, of course. They got into the garage, handcuffed the Dinkleys, and took them away. I sometimes wonder if Danielle and Dave ever worked out that the voices and sirens that had made them give up hadn't been the police at all. That all of them had been Sid. He really is a great ventriloquist. And he'd just given the performance of his life.

They'd have been so angry if they knew. The police had come as quickly as they could, once Sid called them. But the Dinkleys could easily have gotten to us — and gotten away clean — before they arrived, if Sid hadn't taken matters into his own hands. Or hand, as Jacko put it.

The police had called Mom, Sunny's mother, and Timmy's parents. They all arrived in a panicky bunch just as the police van left.

Sid was the hero of the day. He stood in the magic shop with Jacko on his good arm, surrounded by his fans.

"We can't thank you enough," Mom told Sid, "for rescuing Tom. How did you know he was in the garage?"

"I heard him," said Sid simply. "I was hanging around in the shop, see. I was sort of keeping an eye out for Dave and Danielle, waiting for them to get back from their walk. Just after they came in the back gate, I heard Tom yell my name. That was enough for me. I called the cops. Then I went out for Tom."

He grinned at Sunny and Timmy. "He didn't really need me, of course, from what I hear. He had Wonder Woman and Timmy the Terrible to protect him."

Sunny's mother laughed and Sunny looked embarrassed, but Timmy pushed out his chest and his parents beamed with pride. I groaned to myself. There'd be no holding back the kid now.

"Sid," I accused, "you mean you knew all the time that Dave and Danielle were doing the Gripper robberies?" I said.

"Oh, no. I didn't start suspecting them till yesterday. The sketch you showed me tipped me off. I knew that face was one of my old masks. Dave and Danielle could have taken it from the storeroom at any time when they came in through the back door of the shop."

"But anyone could have bought one of those masks," Sunny said.

"I guess they could," Sid shrugged. "But not lately. They were old stock. I haven't sold one in years. I was afraid you'd show the sketch to the police, Tom, and they'd suspect *me*," he added with a laugh. "Can you imagine that: *me*, Jack the Gripper?"

"No, not really," I said, smiling uncomfortably. I knew I could never tell him that for a few mad moments I actually *had* imagined it. Very clearly.

"But anyway, it wasn't just the mask, the mask just started me thinking. About the Dinkleys. How harmless and respectable they looked. How they went for that walk every night. How the Gripper attacks had started around the time they took the apartment."

He grinned. "And then there was Danielle herself, and her smocks, and the so-called baby on the way. I thought about how in all the time she'd been here, she didn't seem to get any bigger. When they took the apartment four months ago, she looked like she was ready to have a baby any minute. When she said the baby wasn't due for a few more months, I thought, Hang on, is she having a baby or an elephant? But I put it out of my mind till last night."

"At the end of this week, they'd have been off and away," I said. "Lucky we caught them when we did."

"Otherwise for sure they'd be lying low for a while, then starting up business somewhere else," Sunny's mother put in.

"At least their business pays, Sid," said Jacko. "Unlike some."

"Crime doesn't pay, Jacko," said Sid sternly.

"Oh, yes. I forgot. Sorry, Sid."

❀

The good news is that very soon after that, Sid's Magic and Games became the hottest business in Raven Hill. Kids came from everywhere to buy games and to see Sid in his magician's outfit and to listen to Jacko's corny jokes.

Elmo's dad wrote a front-page article for the *Pen* about Sid, with a headline that read:

SID'S MAGIC GRIPS THE GRIPPER

In no time, Sid's face was in newspapers and magazines all over the country, and even on TV.

Money and fame didn't change him, though. He went on just as before. Like I said to Sunny, Sid really isn't your average person.

But there were two more mysteries to be solved: Who stole Jonathon's photo money? Well, I'm sorry, but nobody knows that to this day. And as for the mysterious "magic" money that helped Sid finance his shop's new look? Simple, a loan from the bank. And now that's all paid off.

Help-for-Hire Inc. got lots of credit, of course, and that was great for business. But one person who deserves special mention is Timmy. When it came to itching powder, that kid really was creative after all.

Want to know what happens next?
Here's a sneak peek from:

EMILY RODDA'S
RAVEN HILL MYSTERIES

CASE #3: BEWARE THE GINGERBREAD HOUSE

Beware the Gingerbread House

Dressing up as a rabbit to sell cakes isn't my idea of a sensible job. But Help-for-Hire Inc. has said yes to crazy jobs before, and I've never objected.

I guess that was why Liz, Tom, Elmo, Nick, and Richelle were so surprised when I said I didn't want to work at the Gingerbread House.

"I can't *understand* you, Sunny Chan," Liz shrieked. "You go along with all sorts of boring, yucky jobs when we're overloaded. And then a dream chance comes along just when we really need it, and you say no!"

She waved her hands at the kids streaming out of the school yard. "Don't you realize that there isn't a single person at Raven Hill High who wouldn't give an arm and a leg for this?"

"There is, as a matter of fact," I said. "Me."

Nick and Richelle looked at each other, and Richelle rolled her eyes. They didn't mean for me to see, of course, but I did. I stared at Richelle, and she just blinked at me lazily without smiling, and flicked back her long blond hair.

"I don't think I'd give an arm *and* a leg, actually," Tom said, with his face all screwed up as though he was really considering it.

"Oh, shut up, Tom!" shouted Liz. "This is serious. Without Sunny, we're a person short. Mrs. Crumb wants six rabbits. Six! And I told her we'd do it. I never dreamed anyone would object. Good money, a chance to show everyone how reliable we are again — and all that cake and stuff for free!"

Tom moaned softly to himself. He dug around in his pocket and found a half-eaten Snickers bar. It was a bit melted at one end, but he started chewing on it anyway.

Liz put her hands on her hips and glared at me. "Sunny, as far as I know, you haven't even been *inside* the Gingerbread House," she said. "How do you know you won't like it?"

My heart thudded. "I have been in it," I said, pleased that my voice sounded as level as usual. "A year ago, when it first opened."

"Well, then you know it's fabulous. So give me *one* good reason why you don't want the job," Liz demanded.

I couldn't tell her the truth. I just couldn't. And none of them would have believed me if I did. So I took a breath, looked straight into Liz's worried hazel eyes, and lied.

"I'll give you three good reasons," I said firmly. "One, I don't want to dress up in some stupid rabbit costume. Two, my father's arriving from Australia tomorrow for the school vacation, and I want to spend some time with him. Three, I don't like cake."

"Well, *that's* not a problem," Tom put in cheerfully. "You can give your share of the goodies to me."

"If anyone thinks *I* want to wear one of those gross rabbit costumes, they're wrong," remarked Richelle, inspecting her fingernails with a frown. "Those big teeth! And the starey eyes! Yuck! And *I* certainly won't be eating lots of cake — everyone knows *I* don't eat fattening food. It's just that *I* happen to want Help-for-Hire Inc. to go on. *I* don't want to be selfish and let everyone else down."

"Besides, you owe your mother a fortune because of those boots you got, and you need the money," I couldn't help saying. I wasn't going to let Richelle get away with pretending to be unselfish for the first time in her life.

Liz sighed heavily.

At this point, Elmo decided it was time to move off the side-lines and do his part for peace. "If Sunny doesn't want the job, we could always get someone else to stand in for her," he said.

It was a sensible suggestion, but I knew Liz wouldn't go for it.

Sure enough, she frowned. "We can't do that!" she objected. "We're supposed to be a team. A reliable team. Once we start letting strange kids in, the whole point of Help-for-Hire Inc. will disappear. And now — especially now — we have to show every-one we're still a strong group."

She bit her lip and looked at me reproachfully. I knew what was behind that look. *Why are you doing this, Sunny?* she was think-ing. *You're my best friend. You're always so calm and sensible. I've always been able to depend on you.*

I hated disappointing Liz. Our part-time job agency was her baby. She'd thought of it when we all needed to make some money. She'd gotten us organized enough to advertise as a group. She'd really worked hard to get us started.

And we'd all done well so far, too. Sure, we'd gotten into a bit of trouble along the way. A few of our jobs had gotten us mixed up in mysteries and adventures — a couple of them quite dangerous. But that was half the fun. I thought so, anyway, though Richelle was always complaining about it.

But now Help-for-Hire Inc. was in a different kind of trouble. Trouble that wasn't fun. And I knew this wasn't the time to back out of a good job. Especially when my real reason for not wanting to work in the Gingerbread House didn't make any sense at all.

"We'll lose the gig if we don't make up our minds soon," Nick's cool voice put in. "The Work Demons would jump at it. And there are six of them."

Elmo and Liz scowled ferociously at the very mention of the Work Demons — this other group from Raven Hill High who'd copied our Help-for-Hire idea and were going around everywhere trying to scoop up all the best jobs.

But it was the thought of losing all that free food at the Gingerbread House that sent Tom over the edge. He threw himself down on one knee and held up his hands to me. A group of girls walking past stared at him and giggled behind their hands.

"Sunny, we've been through thick and thin together," he wailed. "Mainly thin. I beg of you, don't fail us now. Come with us to the Gingerbread House. We need you to protect us from the wicked witch."

I ignored him, but it did no good. He just raised his voice to a sort of trembling scream. "Oh, and think of the big, fluffy muffins, and the cream puffs, and the little tiny meringues that melt in your mouth," he begged. "Not to mention the chocolate truffles. They don't want to fall into the greedy paws of the Work Demons, Sunny. They want us. They want *me*!"

"Tom, get up," I said severely. But I could feel my mouth starting to curve into a grin. I couldn't help it. Tom always makes me laugh.

"Everyone's staring at you, Tom," hissed Richelle, turning away and trying to look as though she didn't belong with us.

He took no notice. He could see that I was weakening. He dragged himself toward me, still on one knee, and started tugging at the hem of my shirt. He looked ridiculous.

I just stood there, feeling helpless. Liz was running her hands through her hair in frustration. Elmo was grinning all over his freckled face. Nick — Mr. Cool — was looking disgusted. Richelle was edging even farther away from the embarrassment. Everyone was staring at us.

Why am I doing this? I thought suddenly. *Why am I causing all this fuss? I'm being idiotic. Childish.*

Suddenly, the fight didn't seem worth it.

"Oh, all right!" I said, half laughing and half angry, batting Tom's clutching hand away. "I'll do it! Now are you satisfied?"

To be continued . . .

A crime spree chock-full of surprises.

EMILY RODDA'S
RAVEN HILL MYSTERIES

#3: BEWARE THE GINGERBREAD HOUSE

■SCHOLASTIC

After starting a job agency to earn extra money, these six thirteen-year-olds are now uncovering some of their town's most mysterious secrets and finding themselves wrapped up in a lot of trouble. Their most recent assignment at a pastry shop seems like a sweet dream until jewel heists begin nearby.

Welcome to Raven Hill...where danger means business.

■SCHOLASTIC